At the first si[g] **Jude knew tha[t]** **cover, her maga[zine would] break all the sales recor[ds]**

It was as though the Marlboro Man had suddenly stepped down from a billboard.

"Hello, Lucky. I've heard a lot about you from your sister."

"Ma'am." His voice was deep and rough.

He was wearing ebony boots polished to a sheen, jeans and a low-crowned silver-gray cowboy hat. "Why don't you take off that shirt?" she suggested.

"What?" He was looking at her in the same way an old-time movie sheriff might look at the desperadoes who'd just ridden into town with bank robbing on their minds.

"Didn't your sister explain?" When Lucky continued to frown, Jude outlined their crisis. How the cover model had eloped and *he* was the replacement.

Lucky crossed his arms. "I'm not going to take off my clothes for the entertainment of thousands—"

"Millions," Jude interjected in the interest of full disclosure. "We've gone international."

"No. Whenever I take off my clothes in front of a woman, there's just the two of us." He smiled at her and Jude felt in imminent danger of sensory overload. "Call me old-fashioned...."

The author of over fifty novels, **JoAnn Ross** wrote her first story—a romance about two star-crossed mallard ducks—when she was just seven years old. She sold her first romance novel in 1982 and now has over eight million copies of her books in print. Her novels have been published in twenty-seven countries, including Japan, Hungary, Czech Republic and Turkey. JoAnn married her high school sweetheart—twice—and makes her home near Phoenix, Arizona.

Look for her next Temptation novel, *1-800-HERO*, in August.

Books by JoAnn Ross

HARLEQUIN TEMPTATION

Don't miss any of our special offers. Write to us at the following address for information on our newest releases.

Harlequin Reader Service
U.S.: 3010 Walden Ave., P.O. Box 1325, Buffalo, NY 14269
Canadian: P.O. Box 609, Fort Erie, Ont. L2A 5X3

HUNK

OF THE MONTH

JoAnn Ross

Harlequin Books

TORONTO • NEW YORK • LONDON
AMSTERDAM • PARIS • SYDNEY • HAMBURG
STOCKHOLM • ATHENS • TOKYO • MILAN
MADRID • WARSAW • BUDAPEST • AUCKLAND

With thanks to
Lori Walck, Carole Howey and Roger Fowler
for filling in the blanks

ISBN 0-373-25783-X

HUNK OF THE MONTH

1

"WHERE IN THE WORLD am I going to find a man willing to take his clothes off for me in the next forty-eight hours?"

Jude Lancaster dragged her hands through pale blond hair that was in dire need of a trim. She'd missed two haircut appointments in the past ten days. After the second, Rudolfo himself had called her Madison Avenue office, suggesting that if she didn't care enough about her appearance to get her derriere down to his Rudolfo's On Fifth salon, perhaps she should allow someone else to take her slot. Someone, perhaps, who could manage her life better.

Oh, he hadn't actually said all that, but Jude had heard the accusation in her hairdresser's frosty tone, just the same. She had, of course, apologized profusely. She'd even offered to pay for the missed appointments, a gesture he'd haughtily refused. But it hadn't changed the facts. The sorry truth was that she—an admitted control freak—seemed incapable of managing anything about her life these days. Including *Hunk of the Month* magazine.

Which brought her back to the crisis at hand. "It's a good thing Harper's in the Himalayas right now," she muttered. That was another thing she couldn't understand. What kind of man went backpacking in the middle of nowhere on his honeymoon? "Because if he was anywhere I could reach him, I'd track him down and shoot him."

"You're antigun," her assistant, Kate Peterson, reminded her.

"I think I've just become an NRA convert."

On second thought, Jude considered, shooting was too good for the male model who'd been signed to be the featured centerfold hunk for the issue that was to go to press in a mere six weeks.

Factoring in the time needed for Zach Newman, the photographer she'd signed to shoot a layout to go along with the copy extolling the Wild West life-style, she needed to find a replacement in the next two days. Otherwise the new publisher—a take-no-prisoners Australian dubbed Tycoon Mary by the press and those unfortunate enough to work for her—would undoubtedly demote Jude right back to the editorial assistant job she'd had when she'd started working for the magazine right out of college.

No, a gun was too quick for the likes of Harper Stone. A weedwhacker, Jude decided evilly. And she knew just what part of his anatomy she'd begin with. It was the first pleasant thought she'd had all day.

"Did you manage to get hold of Aaron?" Aaron Freidman was the hunk's shark of an agent. The same shark who'd been pressuring her for nearly a year to put his client on the cover of the popular women's magazine.

"His secretary said he's with a client."

Jude lifted a disbelieving pale brow. "All day?"

Hah! It was far more likely Aaron was hiding out to avoid her wrath. *Coward,* she thought scathingly, adding the fast-talking, Armani-wearing agent to her fantasy weedwhacker list.

"The client's on a *GQ* shoot in Milan. He's afraid of flying, so Aaron went with him, to hold his hand, so to speak." Kate slumped down in the molded white suede chair on the visitor's side of the immaculate glass-topped desk in Jude's office.

"If it's any consolation, the secretary said Aaron was as surprised by Harper's elopement as we are," Kate revealed. "Apparently it was a spur-of-the-moment decision. A romantic weekend that turned into something more serious."

"I hate romance." Jude took a swallow of cold coffee. "My only consolation is the thought that this might kill his career. How many women are going to be willing to stand in line for hours at Wal-Mart for one of his autographed books now that they can't fantasize about him?"

"I'm not sure marriage and fantasies are mutually exclusive," Kate suggested carefully. "I mean, being married hasn't hurt Tom Cruise. Or Mel Gibson, or—"

"I get the point," Jude snapped, then immediately wished she hadn't when a wounded puppy dog look appeared in Kate's soft brown eyes. It constantly amazed her that such a gentle-hearted person would have chosen to work in a business definitely not known for sensitivity.

"I'm sorry. It's just been a rotten day." Week. Month. Year. If she weren't addicted to innerspring mattresses and indoor plumbing, she might consider running off to the Himalayas, too.

"You've been under a lot of stress this year, what with the management takeover and all," Kate said sympathetically. "I was thinking...perhaps we could book Kyle Calder."

It wasn't a bad suggestion, Jude thought. Especially

since Kyle was Harper's chief rival in the world of romance novel cover hunks. It would, admittedly be a lovely bit of revenge. Except for one little thing...

"Calder's upcoming cover is for a pirate book."

"Pirates are sexy," Kate argued. "In fiction, anyway. Blackbeard, of course, according to reports, was not at all charming, but I've read a lot of great pirate romances."

Jude was not surprised to learn that Kate read romance novels. If there was ever a woman who believed in happy endings, it was Kate O'Neill Peterson. There were times when Jude almost envied her editorial assistant for her starry-eyed, rose-colored view of the world. But then reality—like Harper The Rat Stone screwing up her schedule—would come crashing down on her and she was grateful to be a card-carrying pessimist.

"The copy's already been written for Harper's cowboy segment in the collector's issue," Jude reminded Kate. "With the new subscription quotas Tycoon Mary has set, we need something that'll top last year's cops and firemen."

That one had gone skyrocketing through the roof—outselling the previous year's construction worker collector's issue—which had succeeded in raising the bar even higher. After six years in the business, there were times, and this was definitely one of them, when Jude felt exhausted from playing publishing limbo.

"And although I could cheerfully kill him, the fact remains that Harper's currently the hottest hunk in fringed buckskin. Factor in the upcoming release of his latest ghostwritten old-time Tombstone novel, and we've got a built-in audience...."

"The seventies are hot right now," she mused

grimly. "Maybe we can get the cowboy from the Village People to take off his clothes for us."

"They're in Germany filming a commercial. Mary Hart had the story on 'ET' last night," Kate elaborated when Jude shot her a surprised look.

Kate sighed. Jude sighed. The two women stared glumly at each other. A silence as gloomy as the tarnished silver rain clouds outside the wall of windows settled over them.

Kate was the first to break it. "What if we were to use a real cowboy?"

"Good idea." Damn. There'd been an instant there when Jude had allowed herself a ray of hope. Which was, she'd discovered with a deep inner sigh, always a mistake. Her chances of locating a cowboy in Manhattan were on a par with being struck by lightning.

"Why don't you run out and find us one?" She glared down at the Movado watch she'd bought herself as a reward for her most recent—and it appeared final—promotion. "We've got about forty-three hours left to set up a new shoot."

It irritated her further that her original plan had, indeed, been to spotlight a real cowboy, perhaps one from the national rodeo circuit, until that fateful day her nemesis had lunched at the Four Seasons with Aaron Freidman.

Jude had no idea what the agent had said to seduce the magazine's publisher into overriding her managing editor; all she knew was the Tycoon had returned to the office, scrapped the initial concept and announced they were going with Harper Stone.

"Actually," Kate ventured carefully, "I was thinking of Lucky."

"Lucky?" Jude lifted a blond brow. "Your brother Lucky?"

"He's pretty cute."

"If that picture you have on your desk is even close to reality, he's drop-dead gorgeous. But I thought he never left Death Valley."

"Cremation Creek."

"Whatever." Jude waved the correction away with an impatient hand. "My point is that you had to take Dillon back to Montana because your brother wouldn't even come to New York to meet his new nephew."

"Cremation Creek is in Wyoming. And he would have come, but I was a little homesick anyway, so it made more sense to take Dillon back to the ranch.

"And you're right about Lucky not being real wild about cities. But that will work in our favor, because it's his country beliefs—sort of his own personal Code of the West—that makes him take his role of big brother seriously."

"Now that you mention it, I seem to recall something about him threatening Jack with a shotgun wedding when you got pregnant."

Soft pink color rose in Kate's cheeks. "He was a little upset," she conceded. "But once Jack assured him that he was going to, as Lucky so succinctly put it, make an honest woman of me—"

"You're kidding." Jude shook her head in disbelief and found herself smiling for the first time since she'd gotten the bad-news phone call first thing this morning. "He actually used those words? What century does your brother live in, anyway?"

"He may be a bit old-fashioned," Kate conceded. "But he *is* cute."

And that, Jude reminded herself, was the key. "He's also in Montana."

"Wyoming. And I can get him to come here."

"How?"

"I'll lie."

"You'd do that? For the magazine?"

"No." Kate lifted her small, clefted chin. "I'd do it for you. You've been more than a mentor since I came to work here, Jude." Her velvety brown eyes were more earnest than Jude had ever seen them. "If you hadn't lobbied so hard for that in-house day care center, I don't know what I would have done because it would have broken my heart to leave Dillon alone all day with some nanny. Next to Jack, you're my very best friend. I'd do anything to help you."

It was, Jude realized, the truth. Even more surprising was how she'd come to feel the same way about Kate. That thought brought to mind something her father had told her when he'd first taken her to his office on her seventh birthday in lieu of the slumber party with friends that she'd asked for.

"Business people don't have friends, Jude," he'd proclaimed in the same voice she'd imagined God must have used when dictating the Ten Commandments to Moses. "They have interests."

And as much as she'd admittedly enjoyed running the photocopier and having a birthday luncheon on the damask-draped table in the executive dining room of the international publishing house, a very strong part of Jude had wished she'd been home playing Barbie dolls with Peggy Jo McBride and Amy Van Pelt.

Her father had taught her everything she knew about the publishing jungle. And since her mother had died before Jude's fifth birthday, he'd also been the one to teach her about life. Which, admittedly, in his rigid, workaholic viewpoint, had been synonymous with work. But this past year working with Kate had proven to Jude that he'd been way off the mark when it came to mixing friendship and business.

Conning Lucky O'Neill into coming to Manhattan was admittedly a long shot. But her father had also taught her that the greatest risks also often earned the greatest rewards. Besides, it wasn't as if she had a plethora of choices, Jude reminded herself grimly.

"What the hell." She handed Kate the receiver of the sleek ivory desk phone, then punched nine for an outside line. "I suppose it's worth a try."

And there was always the chance that a real, down-to-earth, rough-and-tumble cowboy might prove even more popular with readers than a bulked-up cover model who was, quite frankly, already in danger of becoming overexposed.

Jude wondered if Harper had figured that out and decided to pull this disappearing act to boost interest in himself. Whatever. As far as *Hunk of the Month* magazine was concerned, Harper was old news. One thing her father had been right about was that a magazine was a lot like a shark—if it didn't keep moving, it died. Or worse yet, got eaten by an even larger shark.

Jude pictured the framed snapshot on Kate's cluttered desk and envisioned stripping the faded chambray shirt and jeans from the man grinning down from the back of his horse. She imagined Lucky O'Neill clad in a cowboy hat and boots and perhaps a pair of fringed leather chaps.

Oh yes, Jude thought, allowing herself another uncharacteristic burst of optimism. It just might work.

NEARLY A CONTINENT AWAY, oblivious to the plot being concocted against him, Lucky O'Neill scrunched down in his saddle and tried to ignore the rain dripping off the brim of his Stetson.

He'd spent the past twelve hours fixing fences and although it certainly wasn't his favorite thing to do, with summer soon drawing to a close it was time to separate the bulls from the cows so none of the baby heifers got bred. A yearling was too young to calve, and the ones that did get pregnant never grew up to be productive cows.

Knowing how determined a male could get when he was interested in a willing female, Lucky was equally determined to keep that from happening.

It had been a good summer, all things considering. After a wet spring, June and July had turned dry and warm, which made for hay that'd be as sweet as wine for the stock on the cold winter days that were just around the corner. The grass in the upper meadows, where a few stalwart wildflowers continued to bloom, was high and plentiful.

But the afternoon thunderstorms that had been cropping up as August had edged toward September were worrisome. Lightning fires had been burning all over the west, but fortunately, so far southern Wyoming had been spared. Last year a ranch down by Laramie had been partly burned and although Lucky knew that in the long run the range may well be improved by the impact of the blaze, he'd just as soon forgo the experience.

Ranching was a tough business, and most years financially unrewarding. Yet even wet and saddle weary as he was, as he headed back to the ranch, Lucky was extremely grateful to his great-great-grandfather's vision in having settled in the grassy valley along the banks of Cremation Creek in the first place.

After getting his horse—a sweet-tempered bay named Annie—settled down for the night, Lucky headed toward the welcoming yellow lights of the seventy-five-year-old clapboard house. The aroma of beef stew, more enticing than expensive French perfume, welcomed him as soon as he opened the kitchen door.

"Lord, that does smell good," he said to the man seated at the pine table crafted by his great-grandfather from pine grown and milled on the O'Neill's mountain. He lifted the lid on the stew pot. "I think we're ready to bring the bulls down next week."

Buck O'Neill, Lucky's grandfather, looked up from the latest issue of *Western Rider*. "Gotta almost feel sorry for the poor sons of guns. There wasn't a fence built that could have kept me from your grandma. I felt like I'd been poleaxed the first time I saw my pretty young Josie."

Josephine O'Neill had been a beautiful old woman, too. "Your taste in women was as good as it is in horse-flesh," Lucky said.

"Josie was the best-lookin' gal in Wyoming," Buck agreed. "Kate called from her office," he announced, abruptly changing the subject. "Twice."

Lucky stopped in the act of spooning out a bowl of the rich brown supper. His grandfather's announcement was surprising, since he'd talked to his sister only two days ago. They'd always been close, even after she'd moved back east to go to college, then married that blue-blooded investment banker.

"Is everything all right?"

"She wouldn't say." Buck's blue eyes turned thoughtful as he looked up at Lucky over the rim of his chipped coffee mug. "But it sounded like she might've been crying."

"Crying?" Kate had never been a crybaby. He'd seen her fall off many a horse and climb right back on with not so much as a whimper. If she was crying, something was seriously wrong.

"Either that or she's come down with a cold. Which wouldn't be surprising, all those folks breathing the same dirty air." Buck was not a fan of cities. None of the O'Neills had been, until Kate. "The second time she called, she said she was going home and you could reach her there."

"Hell." Giving the bowl a look of regret, he placed it on the wooden counter, pulled a beer from the refrigerator, took the receiver from the wall phone and dialed the familiar number.

"H-hello?" His grandfather was right. Kate had been crying. Lucky could tell from that little hitch in her voice.

"It's me."

"Oh, Lucky!"

It was a wail. One he remembered hearing for the first time when she'd been stood up for the Frontier Day rodeo dance by Cody Murdock. Lucky had, of course driven straight to the Murdock spread and punched Cody's seventeen-year-old lights out. As any big brother would.

"What's the matter? Is it Dillon?"

"N-n-no." He heard a sniffle. "It's Jack."

As hard as he tried for his sister's sake, Lucky had never really taken to his brother-in-law. Jack Peterson was too slick. Too smooth. Too damn eastern.

"What's he done now?" Truthfully, the only thing he could honestly fault Jack with was getting Kate pregnant. But although the Wall Street banker had done the right thing and married her, in Lucky's eyes, that had been crime enough.

"Oh, Lucky," she wailed again, sounding for all the world like a six-year-old who'd just had her dog die on her. "He's l-l-left me."

On some distant level, Lucky experienced surprise that the old expression was true—blood did, indeed, boil. He'd always considered himself a pretty easy-going guy, everyone in Laramie County would attest to the fact that Lucky O'Neill didn't rile easily. But right now he could cheerfully put a bullet through Jack Peterson's black heart.

He didn't waste time asking questions. Didn't push for an explanation, since as far as he was concerned, there was no good reason for a husband to run out on his wife and new baby. Lucky acted as he so often did, as his great-great-grandfather Garvey and every one of the O'Neill men after Garvey had, on instinct.

"There's a flight from Cheyenne to Denver that connects in Las Vegas with the red-eye to New York." He'd checked into the airline schedule when he'd thought he was going to have to fly back east to convince Jack to marry Kate. "If I leave right now, I'll be able to make it.

"You stop crying, honey. Tears never solved a thing and Dillon needs his mama to be strong right now. I'll be there in the morning and fix everything."

And Jack Peterson would be back in the loving bosom of his family by nightfall if Lucky had to go down to that damn high-rise office tower, lasso him like an obstinate steer, hog-tie him and drag him kicking and bawling back to his wife.

"Th-thank you, Lucky." Another sniffle. "I knew I could count on my big brother."

"You can bet the ranch on that one, baby sister." After a few more words of reassurance, he hung up the phone—taking care not to slam the receiver down in case she noticed—and turned to Buck. "The son of a bitch deserted her."

"I never did trust that guy. His eyes are too close together. Ever notice how he squints? And he drinks white wine." In Buck O'Neill's view, this was definitely suspect. "Not to mention him being a banker." Having come too close to losing the family ranch to foreclosure a time or two, Buck considered any banker to be lower than a rattlesnake in a rut.

"You should have shot him when he moved her into his place without marrying her first," the older man said sagely. "And getting her in the family way should have been a hanging offense."

"Well, it's too late for second-guessing the situation now," Lucky said. Above all, a rancher had to remain pragmatic to survive. "Jack Peterson made his bed. Now I'm going to make damn sure he stays in it. Where he belongs."

He stabbed a chunk of beef. It was, as expected, tender and delicious. His grandfather might possess some unbending rules about the natural roles of men and women, but the old man could flat-out cook.

"You oughta take time to eat."

"I don't want to miss my plane." He ate another bite standing at the counter, then took the beer with him as he left the kitchen to pack. He wouldn't need much. After all, there wasn't any way he was going to spend the night in New York City.

He'd calm Katie down, go confront Peterson at his

office, threaten to break every bone in the banker's body, then, after his brother-in-law had seen the light, he'd catch the afternoon flight back to Wyoming and be home at Cremation Creek in time to bring in the bulls.

"WELL, IT'S DONE." Back home in her apartment overlooking the leafy green environs of Central Park—which was as close to nature as a person could get in Manhattan—Kate hung up the phone and turned to Jude. "Lucky's on his way."

"I can't believe you actually lied to him." Jude shook her head in amazement and took another sip of the crisp gold chardonnay.

"It wasn't exactly a lie," Kate argued. Jude wondered which of them she was trying to convince. "Not really. After all, Jack *did* leave."

"Your disgustingly devoted husband went to Boston for a meeting. He'll be home tomorrow. And he's already called you twice this evening."

Although personally, Jude would find such husbandly attentiveness suffocating, she had to admit that it was also rather sweet. From what she'd heard of the conversation between husband and wife at this end, after thirteen months of marriage, Kate and Jack were still billing and cooing like lovebirds.

Despite the seed of guilt that lingered in her eyes, Kate smiled. "He worries."

"So, apparently, does your brother." Jude refilled her wineglass. Since Kate was nursing Dillon, she'd stuck to mineral water.

"Lucky's always been a rock. As solid as granite and every bit as hard to move. Family—and the ranch—have always been the two things he truly cares about.

And I told you, he takes his big brother responsibility very seriously."

"So, what's he going to do when he discovers you set him up?"

Red flags were suddenly flying at full mast in Kate's cheeks. "Oh, I'm certain when I explain how important this is, he'll understand," she said quickly. A bit too quickly, Jude thought. The guilt in Kate O'Neill Peterson's eyes was joined by concern. As if suddenly realizing the enormity of her ruse, she seemed almost relieved when Dillon began to cry.

As Kate escaped the living room, Jude could only hope that she knew what she was doing. Then again, what could happen? she asked herself with a mental shrug.

The worst case scenario would have Lucky O'Neill losing his temper at having been duped. Since the magazine publishing world tended to be populated by more than its share of oversize egos and thin skins, temper tantrums were not uncommon. Fortunately, Jude had become an expert at smoothing ruffled feathers.

Surely a simple cowboy—even an angry one—wouldn't prove all that difficult to handle.

2

LUCKY WAS EXHAUSTED by the time he'd settled into the seat on the flight to New York. The commuter flight from Cheyenne to Denver had been a white knuckler, even for someone who believed man was meant to fly. Which Lucky didn't. Unfortunately, the one from Denver to Las Vegas had been even worse as the plane had bucked like a bronc with a burr under its saddle through a thunderstorm that had required the cabin crew to spend most of the flight buckled into their seats.

There was something unnatural about sitting thirty-thousand feet in the air, surrounded by an oversize tin can, putting your trust in some guy—or woman, these days, he allowed—you'd never even met.

It wasn't really that he was a control freak, Lucky assured himself as the jet taxied down the runway. A rancher couldn't hope to control his environment in a business where so much depended on the weather, fate or God's often bizarre sense of humor. But he still felt a lot more secure atop a horse than he did in an airplane.

The flight attendant on the final leg of the flight was a willowy woman who appeared to be in her early thirties, with a pert red hairdo that swung against her cheekbones, slanted cat's eyes outlined in kohl and glossy red lips that matched her scarf. The gold band on her finger revealed she was married, making him wonder if her husband minded her gallivanting all over the country, smiling and serving drinks to strange men. He surely wouldn't like it.

But then again, since he'd be highly unlikely to ever marry such a polished city type—there wasn't all that much need for silk scarves and lip gloss in Cremation Creek—Lucky decided it was a moot point.

The idea of marriage got him thinking about Kate again. He almost wished he believed in divorce; then he could just bring Kate and Dillon back to Cremation Creek where they belonged and the hell with that skunk his sister had married. Although there'd never been a divorce in the O'Neill clan, Lucky figured that it wouldn't be the end of the world if his sister's marriage did break up. The only problem was, for some reason Lucky couldn't fathom, she seemed stuck on the guy. Which just went to show there was no explaining the female mind.

"Is something wrong, sir?"

The female voice shattered his dark thoughts, making Lucky realize he'd been scowling.

"Not a thing, ma'am." He flashed her his friendliest grin. The one that had worked wonders with women during his college rodeoing days.

"Could I get you a drink? Or a pillow? Or perhaps put your hat in the overhead bin?"

Lucky's fingers instinctively tightened on the brim of his dress gray Stetson. He'd watched the harried-looking businessmen shoving overstuffed carry-on bags and laptop computers into the overhead compartments. There was no way he was subjecting his best hat to that.

"No, thank you, ma'am," he said politely. "I'm just fine."

Her answering smile was friendly. "I thought that's what you'd say. My husband feels the same way about his favorite Resitol. You couldn't get it out of his hands at gunpoint."

"Your husband?" Lucky figured she must be married to one of those fake rhinestone cowboys who liked to dress up in western duds and line dance on Saturday nights.

"He's third-generation rancher. His family has a spread on the front range outside Denver."

This time Lucky's grin was sheepish. That's what he got for tying to pigeonhole people. Still, he was having trouble seeing this sleek woman with the red lips and fingernails castrating bulls and branding calves.

"Nice country."

"We think so." Her cat green eyes had a knowing look that suggested she knew exactly what he was thinking. "Well, I'll leave you to get some sleep."

Worried as he was about Kate, Lucky didn't think that was very likely, but he thanked her just the same.

As it turned out, the long wet day had taken its toll on him and sometime over Kansas, Lucky did indeed fall asleep, not waking up until the pilot announced the plane's descent into New York City.

He stretched in an unsuccessful attempt to work out the kinks earned from spending the night cramped in a too small space, welcomed the warm damp towel the Colorado rancher's pretty wife offered him and enjoyed the lingering memory of a dream of an old-time western necktie party. With that coyote Jack Peterson as the guest of honor.

After making his way through the crowded terminal, where the myriad of voices jabbering away in countless tongues reminded Lucky of the ancient

Tower of Babel, he climbed into a yellow taxi that looked about as banged up as he felt.

He gave the turbaned driver the address of Kate's apartment. Then, remembering his one and only trip to Manhattan for his sister's wedding, Lucky added one vital instruction.

"And take the bridge."

"The bridge is backed up."

"The entire city is probably backed up most of the time. But we're taking the bridge."

He might, on occasion, be forced to fly. But there was no way Lucky was going to risk going beneath the water in some tunnel. If the underwater trap wasn't bombed by damned urban terrorists, it would surely crack from structural damage and drown them all.

His usually easygoing tone was hard. And final. As if sensing he wasn't dealing with his usual fare, the driver glanced up into the rearview mirror, met Lucky's unwavering stare, and then, with a muffled word in some language Lucky couldn't begin to understand, shrugged and pulled away from the curb.

"I told you," the driver said twenty minutes later when they were caught in the tangled snarl of urban gridlock. "I'm going to have to charge you waiting time."

"Fine." Lucky folded his arms and glared back at the dark eyes glowering at him in the mirror. Even breathing toxic exhaust for thirty more minutes was preferable to arriving in the Hereafter soaking wet in a battered yellow cab.

It turned out to be an hour. Which didn't exactly have Lucky in the best of moods when he climbed out of the taxi outside Kate's building.

"May I help you, sir?" Although Lucky towered

over the man dressed in navy blue livery with gold ep-
aulets, the doorman still managed to look down his
nose at him.

"I'm here to see Kate Peterson. Mrs. Jack Peterson."

"Ah, Kate." The doorman surprised Lucky by actually smiling. "She's at work." Despite his surprise that
Kate would be up to going to work after the way she'd
been crying, he was able to catch a hint of the auld sod
in the man's voice. His great-grandfather, who'd died
when Lucky was ten, had the same faint second-
generation American brogue. "But Mr. Peterson is in, if
you'd like to speak with him."

So the skunk had returned. Lucky wondered if he'd
come back for his clothes. Or, perhaps, the storm had
blown over. In which case, he and Peterson still had a
few things to get straight. Like making sure he never
made Kate cry again.

"Yeah. I'd like to speak with Mr. Peterson."

The doorman rang the apartment, then Lucky heard
Jack's voice, instructing the man to send his brother-in-
law up. He certainly didn't sound contrite, Lucky
thought as he took the elevator up to the tenth floor, beginning to get irritated all over again.

The door opened at Lucky's first knock.

"Hey, Lucky." His brother-in-law's handsome face
split in a smile as he stuck out his hand. "What a
sur—"

Lucky cut off the welcome with a quick left to Jack's
jaw. The punch caught Jack Peterson by surprise, sending him reeling backward, where he tripped over a
small wrought-iron-and-wood end table, scattered a
group of miniature enameled boxes, then fell sprawl-
ing on his back on the gray Berber rug.

"What the hell's gotten into you?" Jack glared up at him.

Lucky's temper flared even higher when he realized the skunk didn't even have the gall to look guilty. He strode across the floor to stand over him, hands on his hips as he glared bullets down at the man who'd scrambled to a sitting position and was rubbing his jaw.

"You're just damn lucky I don't shoot you, Peterson." His gaze slid threateningly from his brother-in-law's face. "Or better yet, I should have brought along my nut-cutters. You ever hear of Rocky Mountain oysters?"

When Jack arched an aristocratic blond brow, Lucky had to give him reluctant credit for not groveling. At least the skunk wasn't a coward.

"If you're referring to what I think you are—"

"I'm talking about the leftovers after you turn a bull calf into a steer. Now, you'd probably make a painfully puny serving, but—"

"That's crude, even for you." The other man stood up, his gaze shifting momentarily to the scattered boxes. "Hell, Kate's going to hit the ceiling if anything happened to those. She's been collecting them since her first year at Harvard."

Which was where she'd met this weasel in the first place, Lucky reminded himself, thinking that he should have backed up Buck when his grandfather insisted Kate could get just as good an education at the state university.

"She's got a lot more to be concerned about than a few expensive knickknacks. Like her philandering husband for starters."

"Philandering? I've never looked at another woman since the day I met Kate!"

"Then why did you walk out on her?"

"I didn't." The denial was instantaneous.

Lucky caught hold of the silk tie and pulled Jack closer, so their faces were mere inches apart. "She called me last night, you son of a bitch. In tears."

"Kate was crying?"

"Hell, yes, she was crying. I'd say that was fairly normal behavior for a woman whose husband had deserted her. And their child," he added through clenched teeth. Buck was right. They should have just shot Peterson from the get-go.

"I never deserted her! I never would."

"Are you saying you were home last night?"

"No, but—"

"You're not wriggling out of this." Lucky tightened his grip on the tie.

"I'm not trying to wriggle out of anything, dammit." Although he didn't seem sufficiently contrite, if Peterson's grayish complexion was any indication, he was beginning to get scared. Which was, Lucky decided, a start. "I was in Boston on business. Kate knew that. I called her three times."

"Three times?"

"Once at six, again at eight, before I went out to dinner with clients, then at eleven when I got back to the hotel. It was the first time we've been apart since Dillon was born. I missed her."

Lucky felt his high horse beginning to slip out from under him. If Peterson was telling the truth, and it seemed real strange he wouldn't be, since the story would be easy to check out, the first two calls would have come before he'd called Kate back. This wasn't making any damn sense.

"Kate called me," he insisted darkly, "in tears. Because you'd walked out on her."

"There's no way I'd do that. It'd be easier for me to stop breathing."

Damn. Again, the answer was too quick not to be believed. Which only meant one thing. Kate had obviously lied to him. But why?

"Does she know you're home?"

"No, I just got in."

"Good." Lucky released him. "Let's go."

Peterson straightened his tie. "To her office?"

"Yeah." Lucky stepped over the pretty little boxes on his way back to the door. "I'd say my baby sister has herself some explaining to do."

Lucky ground his teeth on the elevator ride to the lobby, realizing there was no way he was going to escape having to apologize to his brother-in-law. Just one more thing Kate was going to have to answer for, he thought grimly.

"I'm sorry I punched you."

Peterson shrugged shoulders clad in a pinstriped navy suit jacket that Lucky figured cost nearly as much as his best bull.

"I don't have any sisters. But if I did, I would have done the same thing if I'd been in your place."

Until his baby sister had gotten pregnant by this man, Lucky had never been one to hold a grudge. It was, he was realizing now, a tiring way to go through life.

"I think I liked it better when you were a low-down snake of a sister seducer."

"And I was more comfortable thinking of you as

some hick cowboy with manure on your boots and a plug of Redman stuck in your cheek."

"Never chewed tobacco. It's nasty stuff."

The two men observed each other in the close confines of the elevator.

"We're never going to be friends," Lucky warned, just in case Peterson might be thinking otherwise. "We don't have hardly anything in common." Now that was the understatement of the millennium.

"True." Jack rubbed his chin, where a purple bruise was beginning to bloom. "But we do have two very important things in common."

"Kate and Dillon," Lucky said.

"Exactly."

They exchanged another look. And although neither one said the words out loud, the two men from such disparate backgrounds each knew that a tentative peace accord had just been struck.

Fifteen minutes later, they signed in with the guard in the marble-floored lobby, then took the elevator up to the sixty-eighth floor where the executive offices of *Hunk of the Month* magazine were located. When his ears popped, Lucky decided that high-rise buildings were like everything else in this city: about as user friendly as convertible submarines.

The steel doors opened onto a lobby where white slate floors flowed like an arctic ice field and the molded furniture—none of which looked the slightest bit comfortable—was covered in shades of gray, white and black.

"Hi, Megan," Jack greeted the receptionist, who appeared to have dressed to match the room in a sleeveless black linen dress. "We're here to see my wife."

"I'll buzz her and tell her that you're here." As she

reached for the phone, her interested gaze shifted to Lucky.

"Don't bother," Jack said. "We'd prefer to surprise her."

"Fine." From her distant tone, as she continued to stare at him, Lucky decided that his brother-in-law could have informed her that they were mad-dog serial killers come to murder everyone in the building, and she wouldn't have uttered a single word of complaint.

Since she was looking at him as if he were Bigfoot, or some green alien just arrived from Mars, he decided to give the lady what she so obviously expected.

"Howdy, ma'am." The drawl was rich and thick, unlike the way anyone talked in Wyoming. For an added bonus, he touched the brim of his hat.

"Hi." Her voice was a bit breathless. As if she'd just finished climbing those sixty-eight flights of stairs. "Are you a friend of Kate's?"

"I'm her big brother."

She regained her city girl composure quickly. A seductive glint came into gold eyes that took a slow, leisurely tour of him from the brim of the Stetson, down to the pointed toes of his polished Saturday night boots.

"Well, you're certainly that. I can see why Jude decided not to jump out the window after all."

"Jude?"

"*Hunk of the Month*'s managing editor. She was so horribly upset when Harper ran off and got married, leaving her in the lurch. And when Kate came up with her idea, everyone thought it was a long shot, of course, but—"

Internal alarms started blaring inside Lucky with the

urgency of a bull-riding whistle. "What idea was that?"

Her eyes narrowed. "Are you saying you don't know?"

"Know what?"

Lucky was getting more and more frustrated. And confused. He also wasn't at all wild about appearing ignorant in front of this sleek woman who now was observing him with a combination of misgiving and humor.

"I believe I'd better let Kate fill you in," she decided, "when you surprise her." Her gaze slid to Jack. "You remember the way?"

"Yeah." He exchanged a pointed look with his brother-in-law, then headed off down the hall, Lucky right beside him.

The walls of the hallway were lined with enormous framed photos of men in various stages of undress. Although none of them showed full frontal nudity, they sure didn't leave much to the imagination.

Lucky paused in front of a photograph of a fireman posed in front of a shiny red ladder truck, dressed in black rubber boots, helmet and a skimpy pair of dotted briefs that just barely covered the essentials. The guy had his arm around a Dalmatian and wouldn't you just know it, the dog's coat matched the underwear.

"Doesn't it get to you?" he asked.

"What?" Jack paused beside him.

"Having your wife work at a place where she's looking at nearly naked men all day?" Lucky was sure having trouble thinking of his sister working here. Then again, he still hadn't quite gotten used to the idea of her having sex on a regular basis. Which she undoubtedly did, now that she was married and a mother.

"Nah. The way I figure it, it's not so bad if hunks like this turn her on. So long as I reap the benefits at the end of the day."

Lucky cringed and rubbed his jaw. "You know, the idea of you getting lucky with my sister is one of those roads I really don't want to go down."

"Sorry. But you did ask."

"Yeah." Lucky had overheard two of the hired ranch hands talking much the same way about taking their girlfriends to see Alan Jackson perform at the state fair. Jackson was a surefire way of getting lucky that night, they'd agreed, trading winks and leers.

"I still don't think I'd like it," he decided.

"Of course you wouldn't. Because you're a throwback to another century." Jack began walking again. "No offense, O'Neill, but you're definitely out of sync with the thinking of modern women."

Lucky figured that was probably the case. He caught a quick glance of a blowup of one of the magazine covers, featuring a buffed-up guy working on the engine of a classic Corvette clad only in a black leather G-string, and decided that if modern men really needed another guy to warm up their women, then the world was in an even sorrier state than he'd thought.

He saw Kate, seated at a small black desk. She had her back to them and was talking on the phone; if he hadn't known it was his baby sister, he wasn't certain he'd recognize the young woman with the tied-back bright red hair and severely cut tobacco brown suit.

"I know it's going to be a problem, Zach," she said, obviously trying to soothe the man on the other end of the phone. "But Jude says that if we all work together...

"Yes, I understand you aren't used to working with

amateur models and I realize it might take a lot longer to get some usable shots, however..."

When Jack cleared his throat, she swiveled the chair around. Then paled and dropped the receiver onto the desk with a clatter.

The way the color had drained from her face assured Lucky that Kate was guilty. Of what, he still didn't know. But the proof of her falsehood was written across her expressive face in bold script.

Lucky picked up the receiver and held it out to her. "Say goodbye, Katie." It was an order—softly couched, but etched in granite.

Her eyes were as huge and white as a horse's who'd just gotten a whiff of smoke; her hand, as she took the receiver from his, was trembling.

"I'm afraid something's come up," she murmured into the phone. "I'll have to get back to you. I promise, ten minutes." She eyed her brother with obvious trepidation. "On second thought, better make it twenty." She exhaled a long, weary breath. "Believe me, Zach, I understand exactly how you feel. It's a difficult situation for all of us."

That said, she hung up. Apparently deciding that Jack was the safer person to deal with at this moment, she turned toward her husband.

"Hi, honey. I hadn't realized you were coming home this morning." The little tremor in her voice matched the one Lucky had noticed in her hands.

"I caught an earlier flight than planned. I missed you," he said simply. "Lucky showed up at the apartment while I was still unpacking."

When he rubbed his visibly swollen chin with chagrin, Kate's attention narrowed in on the dark blue-and-purple bruise.

"Oh, no! He didn't...he couldn't..." She shot her brother an imploring look. "Lucky, please tell me that you wouldn't—"

"I slugged him." Lucky's glower dared her to criticize what, at the time, had seemed appropriate behavior. He rubbed his skinned knuckles and reminded himself that it was, after all, her damn fault for having lied to him in the first place. "For running out on you."

"Oh, God." She buried her distressed face in her hands.

Neither Lucky nor Jack said a word. They just waited. And waited. Then, waited some more.

Finally, as if unable to take the suspense any longer, Kate peeked out from between her fingers. "I suppose I owe you both an explanation."

"That'd be a start," Jack agreed mildly.

"Damn right you do," Lucky said at the same time.

Kate sighed. And lowered her hands. "It seemed like such a good idea, when I first thought of it."

"What?"

Another sigh. She rubbed her temples with her fingers and didn't answer right away. "Perhaps," she suggested cautiously, "it might be best if Jude explained things."

Along with being the woman the receptionist had told him had decided not to jump out the window, Lucky now remembered that Jude Lancaster was also Kate's immediate supervisor at the magazine.

"If someone doesn't explain something in the next five minutes, I'm out of here."

"Oh, you can't do that!" Although he never would have guessed it possible, Kate went even paler. She was now the same white shade as the papers scattered all over her desk. She looked so much like a ghost that

Lucky wouldn't have been at all surprised to be able to put his hand through her face. "Let me just let Jude know you're here...."

She picked up the receiver again.

Again, Lucky plucked it out of her hand. "I had more of an ambush in mind."

"Oh, God," Kate murmured again.

She looked, Lucky thought, as if *she* were contemplating jumping out a window. He considered assuring her everything would be all right, but decided that after dragging him all the way across the country on what was turning out to be a wild-goose chase, his baby sister deserved to sweat for a while.

She stood up, walked the few feet to a black-lacquered door and knocked.

"Come on in," the female voice, edged with obvious aggravation called out.

Kate entered, flanked on both sides by her husband and brother. "Jude, this is my brother, Lucky. Lucky, this is Jude Lancaster. My boss."

The first thought that flashed through Jude's mind was that Kate definitely hadn't been exaggerating. Her second was that with Lucky O'Neill on the cover, she'd no longer have to worry about making Tycoon Mary's new sales goals.

The candid photograph on Kate's desk hadn't begun to do him justice. It was as though the Marlboro Man had suddenly stepped down from that old billboard in Times Square. But impossibly, this cowboy was even better looking, in an unassuming, naturally sexy way.

"Hello, Lucky. I've heard a lot about you." She kept her voice calm when what she wanted to do was sing hosannas.

"Ma'am." His voice was deep and rough.

Jude stood up, came around her desk and slowly circled Lucky, appraising his potential with an expert eye. He was tall—six foot two, she'd guess—putting his weight around 205 pounds and from what she could see, he was all lean sinew and muscle without an ounce of superfluous fat.

He was wearing ebony boots polished to a sheen a drill sergeant would have admired, stacked jeans, a wide hand-tooled leather belt with a huge gaudy silver-and-gold embossed buckle, a white snap-front shirt, and a low-crowned silver-gray cowboy hat.

Even though she spent her day looking at pictures of near-naked hunks and should be immune to their masculine appeal, Jude suddenly felt in imminent danger of estrogen poisoning.

"Why don't you take off that shirt?" she suggested, forcing her mind back to the business at hand. They were, after all, running out of time. "So I can see what you've got."

Not that she couldn't already. The twill shirt was a trim cut that displayed his body to mouthwatering advantage. Even with his clothes on, he was definitely in the running for the magazine's annual Hunk of the Year award.

"What?"

His brows went crashing toward a nose that looked as if it had been broken. Rather than detract from his looks, it only made him even more sexy.

"As delicious as you admittedly look in that cowboy outfit, I need to check out your credentials, so to speak."

Heaven help her, try as she might, Jude couldn't keep her rebellious eyes from taking a quick, naughty tour downward from his face to where his masculine credentials were enticingly cupped in soft blue denim. If Lucky O'Neill was any indication, it was definitely true what they said about everything being bigger out west.

"It's important to make certain you don't have any scars or tattoos anywhere on your body," she explained as she returned her assessing gaze back up to his strangely stony one.

He was looking at her in the same way an old-time movie sheriff might look at the desperados who'd just ridden into town with bank robbing on their minds. With a great deal of distrust and more than a little dislike.

"Not that any you might have couldn't be concealed with a little computer magic," she assured him quickly, "but—"

"Are you saying you expect me to get naked?"

His still mild tone had taken on a dangerous edge. He shot a lethal, questioning glance at Kate, who had wisely moved out of range and was now standing in front of the floor-to-ceiling corner window.

"Well, not exactly naked," Jude replied, deciding the obvious misunderstanding must be the cause for his glower. "Our editorial policy has always been to leave certain things to our readers' imaginations. However, since you're going to be our Hunk of the Month—"

"I'm going to be what?"

It was a roar. During a long-ago trip to the Serengeti Plain with her father, Jude had heard a lion sound much the same way.

"I haven't had a chance to tell him yet," Kate said in a quiet, miserable little voice.

"Uh-oh." Jude looked at the granite face with the clefted chin that was a larger, rougher version of his sister's and worried that perhaps this simple cowboy might not be as easily handled as she'd originally believed.

"Well, then, in that case, I suppose it's up to me to explain things." She flashed him a bright, professional smile that had always succeeded with everyone but Tycoon Mary. And, apparently, Lucky O'Neill.

His expression didn't change. Ignoring a glower as hot as a branding iron, Jude glanced down at her watch.

"It's nearly lunchtime. Why don't I have Kate book us a table at the Four Seasons, or Lutece, and—"

"No offense intended, ma'am..." Lucky cut her off with a wave of a dark, banged-up hand roughened from years of hard physical work. Despite this latest little glitch in her plans, despite the fact that valuable time was slipping away, Jude found herself wondering if he'd submit to a manicure. "But I'm not real hungry right now. I just want to know what kind of trouble you and Kate have been cooking up."

"Oh, I promise you, Lucky, it's no trouble." She paused, momentarily distracted by the sound of a fire-engine siren coming from the street below. "In fact, if you'd only listen—"

"I'd appreciate it if you could make it short, ma'am." Squint lines fanned out from eyes that were as brown as Bambi's but far more dangerous as he looked at Jude as if sighting down a rifle scope. "Because I have an afternoon flight booked on American Airlines back to Wyoming."

All Jude's pretense at professional calm fled at hearing his plans. She pressed a suddenly ice-cold hand against the front zipper of her suit jacket, trying to forestall the heart attack that was imminent. Down on the street another fire truck raced by, causing her anxiety level to spike even higher.

"Oh, you can't leave!"

"Please, Lucky," Kate said at the same time. "If you'll just sit down and listen to Jude, you'll see that I didn't have any choice."

His eyes softened briefly as they turned toward his sister. But Jude didn't witness any softening of spirit. "There's never any good reason for lying."

"Dammit, that's always been the problem with you, Lucky O'Neill." Kate flared in an uncharacteristic display of temper that had Jude thinking that they'd all become stressed out since Tycoon Mary had blown onto the scene.

"You see everything in terms of black and white," Kate accused hotly. "You've never, in your entire life, been able to see any gray."

"Now there's where you're wrong," he shot back, his own temper firing. "That's all I've been seeing since I got off the elevator. Along with black and white. All except for this office."

The fury in his eyes turned uncharacteristically arctic as his gaze skimmed disdainfully around the room that had cost a fortune to redecorate. "I don't know how anyone could work in here without going snow-blind in the first week."

"White is soothing." Jude defended her color scheme with a toss of her blond head. Although flames were burning behind her rib cage, she was damned if she'd reach for her Tums and give this man—this common cowboy!—the satisfaction of knowing how badly he was upsetting her.

She folded her arms across the front of her dark gray suit and dug her fingernails into palms that practically itched to smack that accusing look off his handsome face.

"I suppose you'd prefer denim? Perhaps Kate could run out to Ralph Lauren—"

"I don't know who this guy Ralph Lauren is, but even a dumb country cowboy can realize when he's just been insulted," Lucky practically growled, once again reminding Jude of a lion. A mountain lion. Like that huge western cougar she'd seen on the Discovery Channel who'd hide behind a big red boulder and pounce on you, just when you least expected it.

She held her ground even as she envisioned her career going down the drain. "I have to point out, Mr. O'Neill, that you threw the first stone, so to speak, when you cast aspersions on my office."

"The name's Lucky," he reminded her. "We're not real comfortable with formality in Cremation Creek. And I wasn't exactly casting aspersions. I only pointed out that your office is white. Real white. But I do apologize if I offended you."

"Thank you." The fire behind the wall of her chest went from a three-alarm blaze to a two. "And I apologize for suggesting that there's anything wrong with denim."

He nodded. "Apology accepted."

"Would you care to sit down?" She gestured toward the alabaster-hued leather Italian sofa. "If you're not ready for lunch, I could have some coffee brought in. Perhaps a few sweet rolls? The deli on the first floor makes the best bagels in town."

"That's real considerate of you, ma'am, but I'm not hungry. And, if you don't mind, after sitting all night on the plane, I'd just as soon stand."

"Whatever you like." Jude felt herself beginning to

relax. Lucky O'Neill's temper might have a very short fuse, but at least it seemed to be fast burning. Now that it appeared to have flamed out, she could get back to convincing him to see the light.

"And you're right, after coming all this way to Manhattan, you're definitely entitled to an explanation." Her smile was back—smooth, friendly, and persuasive. "You see, we'd planned this very special issue..."

3

LUCKY DIDN'T SAY a single word during Jude's careful, lengthy explanation. His expression, which had turned surprisingly inscrutable for a man who earned his living in such a basic manner, didn't change in any way. Watching him carefully, Jude couldn't detect even a flicker of emotion. The quiet strength began to make her even more edgy.

"So," she concluded, "since we were admittedly more than a little desperate, Kate suggested you."

"To be your cowboy Hunk of the Month?"

"That's right. Did I mention it's going to be a collector's issue?" She knew male models who'd run over their best friends for such an opportunity.

"No, I think I would have caught that." He rubbed his square jaw.

In spite of the fact that her only interest in Lucky O'Neill was business, Jude knew she was in serious trouble when she started to imagine those dark hands on her body. The thought caused her blood to run so hot she was amazed she didn't set off the sprinkler system.

It was all the stress she'd been suffering lately, she assured herself. She was merely having a nervous breakdown. The fact that she wanted to drag this hunky cowboy beneath her desk didn't really have anything to do with Lucky O'Neill at all.

"Does that mean more people will buy it?" he asked finally.

"That's our hope." She flashed an encouraging smile. "And, believe me, Lucky, with you on the cover—"

"No way."

"What?" Jude stared at him in disbelief. Hadn't he heard a word she'd said?

"Oh, Lucky," Kate moaned.

Jack didn't say anything. But he did leave Lucky's side to put a comforting arm around his wife.

Lucky folded his arms in front of his snap-front shirt. "I said, there's no way I'm going to take off my clothes for the entertainment of thousands—"

"Millions," Jude interjected in the interest of full disclosure. "We've gone international."

"I'm not undressing in public. Whenever I take off my clothes in front of a woman, there's just the two of us in the room. Call me loco, but I'd prefer to keep certain things intimate."

"But you're so perfect."

"I'm just a cowboy. Not some fancy high-priced male model with manicured fingernails and a fifty-dollar haircut."

Jude decided, in the interest of regaining control of this situation, to skip the idea of the manicure. She also refrained from telling him that most of the men she knew paid at least a hundred dollars for a haircut.

"Modeling's not all that difficult," she assured him. "We have this marvelous photographer, Zach Newman, we've been working with on the centerfolds that—"

"He might be another Emilie Mannion for all I know," Lucky interrupted. "But he can't turn me into what I'm not. I could put my boots in the oven, too, but that wouldn't make them cookies."

He waded across the snowy carpeting, took hold of his sister's shoulders and kissed her cheek. "Sorry, Katie-did," he said, calling her by her childhood nickname. "But this is one mess I can't bail you out of."

That stated, he started to leave the room, then, as if remembering his manners, turned and touched his fingers to the brim of his Stetson, just the way Mel Gibson had in *Maverick*—but with a lot more insolence than respect. "It was real nice meeting you, Miz Lancaster."

With that obviously blatant lie, he was gone.

"Damn!" Jude slammed her hand down on the glass top of her desk, causing the Waterford vase holding the single lily to tip over. Water spilled, but she was too aggravated to notice.

"Who the hell is Emilie Mannion?" she demanded. Jude thought she knew every photographer in the business.

"I don't know," Kate said on a little hitch of breath that suggested this time her tears might be for real.

Jack hugged his wife closer. "I could go after him." As his eyes cut to the open doorway Lucky had just strode through, he looked as if he'd rather crawl naked down Wall Street at high noon. "Try to make him listen to reason."

"That's not necessary," Jude said. "I'll handle it." Somehow. "That man is the most perfect, mouthwatering male specimen I've seen in all the years I've worked at this magazine and I'm not going to let him get away."

She refused to even consider the fact that she could possibly be harboring personal reasons for wanting to keep Lucky in New York. While there was no denying that sharp, surprising jolt of attraction that had set every atom in her body to spinning dizzily out of control, her response had merely been an attack of lust. A chemical brain bath. Admittedly hotter and more mind-blinding than any she'd ever experienced, but Jude had never been the kind of foolish woman to allow her heart—or her hormones—to overrule her head. So she wasn't about to throw away a lifetime of cautious sexual behavior just because Lucky O'Neill was the kind of man who could make any woman drool.

She opened a white-lacquered filing cabinet, retrieved her purse, took out a key on an embossed silver ring and tossed it to Kate. "In case I can't catch up with him before he leaves for the airport, call American Airlines and get me on whatever flight your brother's taking back to Montana—"

"Wyoming."

Jude shrugged off the correction and, as the fire in her gut escalated into a conflagration, she popped two chalky antacids into her mouth. It really didn't matter where she was headed since Lucky O'Neill was the solution to all her problems. She'd be willing to follow the drop-dead gorgeous cowboy to Timbuktu if that's what it took.

"Whatever. Book two first-class tickets for Zach and me and move your brother out of coach. You can reach me on my cell phone and let me know what flight we're booked on. Next, telephone Zach at his studio and tell him to meet me at the departure gate. Instruct him to bring all the equipment he'll need for an outdoor shoot."

If they were going to use a real cowboy, it only made sense to photograph him in the great outdoors. Besides, Jude doubted there were any studios in the wilds of Montana that would satisfy the perfectionist photographer.

"Finally, if you wouldn't mind, please run by my apartment and pack some appropriate casual clothes and underwear and courier them to your brother's ranch."

Without giving Kate time to respond, Jude scooped up her briefcase containing her laptop computer and strode purposefully out of her office and down the long hallway. On the trail of Lucky O'Neill.

She had not achieved the status of managing editor of a major magazine by allowing a few roadblocks to get in her way. Okay, she admitted, this was more than a mere roadblock. It was more like a moat filled with editor-eating alligators. She and Tycoon Mary hadn't hit it off from the start; she had no doubt that the publisher was just waiting for her to fail so she could replace her with that smarmy nephew she'd installed as vice president in charge of marketing.

Well, that wasn't going to happen, Jude vowed. Lucky O'Neill was going to be her Hunk of the Month. And with the stud-muffin cowboy from Cremation Creek on the cover, sales would skyrocket into the stratosphere, rescuing not only her career, but her hard-won reputation for being on top of the publishing game, just as the legendary John Lancaster had been before her.

Although her father had died last year of a heart attack at a publisher's conference in California—after hitting his ball into the surf during a golf game at Pebble Beach—Jude continued to feel as if she were being judged by his tremendous success. As if she were in competition with her famous parent. Or at least attempting to live up to his impossibly high standards. John Lancaster had been famous—or infamous, depending on your point of view—for maintaining absolute control over everything in his world.

Of course there had been one thing he couldn't control, Jude considered, thinking back on that terrible night of her mother's death. But, as was his way, he hadn't bothered to dwell on the past; he'd moved on and although there had been times Jude had longed to share her loneliness or night fears, she'd intuitively understood that her father would have only told her to straighten up.

That had been, she remembered, his answer for everything. *Straighten up and fly right.* How many times had she heard those words directed her way? How many times had she promised to do exactly that? Too many to count.

As she breezed past the receptionist and punched the Down button for the elevator with more force than necessary, Jude remembered another important lesson her father had taught her: Every man has his price.

"If I can't discover Lucky O'Neill's," she muttered as the elevator descended swiftly to the ground floor, "I'll eat his pretty gray cowboy hat."

LUCKY WAS ANGRY enough to chew tenpenny nails and spit out bullets. What the hell had gotten into Kate, thinking he'd ever consider having his picture taken buck naked? Well, not exactly naked, he allowed, but those blown-up photographs hanging in the hallway of the *Hunk of the Month* offices sure hadn't left all that much to the imagination.

He was still seething when the express elevator reached the lobby. The wedge heels of his boots made a loud clacking on the marble floor as he made a bee-line for the revolving door.

"Lucky!" a familiar voice called out. He ignored it.

"Dammit, Lucky O'Neill!" Moving faster than he would have guessed possible in those ridiculous high heels and short tight skirt, Jude somehow managed to slip into the revolving door behind him. "If you'd only listen to reason..."

Her breasts, which had appeared almost nonexistent beneath the severe cut of her suit, were pressed against his back, her belly shoved up against his butt in a way that was just too intimate for comfort in the narrow space.

He shot her a look over his shoulder. "I've already heard your pitch, ma'am."

"You haven't given me a fair chance."

His momentary lack of attention made him miss the sidewalk, forcing them to go around again.

"I heard you out fair and square. But I'm not buy-ing."

Her scent surrounded Lucky in the close space. Un-like the rest of this godforsaken city, she smelled fresh and clean, reminding him of white cotton sheets dry-ing in a sun-warmed summer breeze. The subtle fra-grance was a lot different from the sweetly floral perfumes favored by most of the buckle bunnies of his acquaintance.

He escaped the door on the second pass, and waved toward a passing taxi. Confirming his belief that this would go down as one of the most rotten days of his life, the driver ignored him. As did the second.

"You might be an expert at rounding up mavericks on the range, cowboy," Jude said when the third cab refused to stop, "but you've got a lot to learn about city life."

Before Lucky could inform her that he had neither the need nor the desire to develop urban survival skills, she stepped off the curb with a total lack of regard for life and limb, stuck her fingers into her mouth and let loose with a piercing whistle.

The ear-shattering sound proved immediately effective; a cab pulled over from the far lane, accompanied by a blare of car horns as it screeched to a halt.

"That was a pretty good trick," he admitted, yanking open the back door before the driver could change his mind. Lucky had always been one to give credit where credit was due.

"If you think that's something, you should see what I can do on rainy days with an outstretched leg." She slid past him, climbing into the back seat with a flashy show of leg. "Well?" She glanced up as he was momentarily distracted by her smooth firm thighs. "Are we going or not?"

"What do you mean, *we*?"

"You're going back to Montana, right?"

"Wyoming."

"Wyoming, Montana." Jude threw up her hands both literally and figuratively. "You and your sister are so damn picky."

"It's not picky to be proud of your roots," Lucky said with a lot more patience than he was feeling. "Montana's the Big Sky State. Wyoming's officially the Equality State. Others call it the Cowboy State, but we like to think our sky's pretty big, too. Where are you from?"

She immediately opted against revealing that her parents had brought their infant girl home to their ten-room apartment on Park Avenue because she feared it would make her sound like a snob at a time when she wanted to win his cooperation. Besides, why should she expect a cowboy to understate the urban island's rigid social order?

"I'm a native New Yorker. I was born right here in Manhattan."

"There you go," he drawled. "So how would you like it if I kept referring to New Jersey as your home?"

"Good point."

The cabbie turned around. "You two gonna talk all day?" he growled around an unlit cigar. "Or you wanna go somewhere? Like to the National Geography Bee, maybe?"

"We're going to the airport." Jude didn't take her eyes from Lucky's as she answered. "La Guardia or Kennedy?"

"Kennedy." Since she'd apparently decided to ride along to press her crazy case again, Lucky shrugged and climbed into the cab beside her. "American Airlines. And take the bridge."

"I truly am sorry about Kate deceiving you that way," Jude said as the cab pulled into traffic.

Lucky didn't trust that contrite, dulcet tone for a minute. "Are you saying you didn't know anything about it?"

"No."

So much for the apology. Her chin came up a notch in a challenging way that reminded him vaguely of someone. But he couldn't put his finger on just who.

Whoever it was, it reminded Lucky that he'd always liked a woman with guts, and Jude Lancaster sure seemed to have more than her share. That sharp thrust-out chin made him want to kiss her stubbornness away. He really must be going loco, he thought, even imagining locking lips with Kate's boss. Lucky wondered how long it took for urban pollution to rot a man's brain.

"I'm merely professing regret about you having been lured here under false pretenses." In a smooth gesture he suspected was meant to undermine his resistance, she placed her hand on his thigh. Her skin was smooth and white, her nails short and unlacquered. "*Hunk of the Month* magazine will, of course, reimburse all your travel expenses."

He'd intended to pluck that seductive hand away but, for some reason he wasn't going to try to figure out, didn't. "That's not necessary. O'Neill men always pay our own way."

"Don't be ridiculous. If Kate hadn't fudged the truth in the first place—"

"It was more than fudging. She flat-out lied." His firm, unbending tone had Jude understanding Kate's accusation that Lucky O'Neill was a man who viewed the world in simple black-and-white terms.

"That's a remarkably rigid attitude to have about your own sister."

"I love Katie to pieces," Lucky said. "There's not a thing I wouldn't do for her. But that doesn't change the fact that what she did was wrong."

"Gotta love that old Code of the West," Jude drawled, not quite able to keep the acid from her tone.

"Now there you go, being sarcastic," he said easily. He was not going to let this sexy smart-mouthed female rile him up. "But the thing is, there really *is* a code. It's not written down anywhere, but where I come from, a man's brought up to know what's right and what's wrong."

Black hats and white hats. Just like in those old movies. Like the Clint Eastwood spaghetti westerns that provided such pleasure on dateless Saturday nights and rainy Sunday mornings. The movies that had been the impetus for the feature article about cowboys in the first place.

"And you believe what we did was wrong." It was not a question.

"Sure I do. And, I figure, deep down inside, you know it, too. But that's all water under the bridge. And there's no point arguing, Miz Lancaster, since I'm not changing my mind."

Jude exhaled a long, frustrated breath. "Has anyone ever told you that you have a very hard head beneath that cowboy hat?"

"It's been mentioned a time or two. But like my grandpa Buck always says, a man who spends too much time straddling the fence only gets a sore crotch."

"Well, that's certainly a pithy bit of western wisdom," she snapped, clearly frustrated.

Her spine went as straight as a lightning rod. He watched as she ran a hand over her palomino pale hair, which fell straight as rainwater past her jaw. Energy radiated from Jude Lancaster's every fragrant pore; she reminded Lucky a lot of quicksilver.

They looked at each other, her frustrated gray eyes meeting his unwavering brown. A challenging silence stretched between them.

Finally, Jude asked, "So who is Emilie Mannion?"

"A western photographer back at the turn of the century. I've got some sepia postcard copies of pictures she shot of the Cheyenne Frontier Days rodeo. Great stuff."

"Oh." She wondered who owned the copyright. Including a few of them—and perhaps posing Lucky in the same way—might add an artistic sense of history to the layout.

Another silence. As he watched her drag her hand through her hair, cross her legs with an impatient swish, wiggle her high-heeled foot, Lucky wondered what it would take to get this woman to unwind. He also wondered if she'd be this animated in bed. An image flashed through his mind—a mental picture of tumbling her in a hayloft while a benevolent summer sun made her lily-white skin glow golden.

Hell. What had gotten into him? This too skinny, fast-talking city slicker wasn't his type. He liked his women warm, lush and willing. He liked them to move slowly and seductively, inside bed and out. Not that he had any intention of taking little Ms. Publishing to bed, he reminded himself. Besides, he doubted there were any convenient haylofts to be found in Manhattan.

"Look, it's not that I really care one way or another whether or not you do the layout," Jude began, her honeyed tone belying her still sky-high blood pressure.

"Aw shucks, ma'am." His voice was smooth, but his eyes had turned granite hard again. "I might just be a dumb old cowpoke, but I'm finding that line a bit hard to swallow."

"It's true." It was, Jude assured herself as the persistent fire in her chest flared over the antacids again, only a little white lie. "I'll undoubtedly get fired if you don't, but to tell you the truth, the job has begun to lose its appeal anyway." That was definitely the truth. "So, starting over might be a good thing for me in the long run, creatively speaking."

As soon as she heard herself saying the words she'd been thinking for so long out loud, Jude realized, with not a little surprise, that she actually meant them.

She'd really have to think about this, she considered. When she had more time. After the collector's issue was put to bed. Which wasn't going to happen unless she could get Lucky O'Neill to agree to be her hunk.

"There's just one little problem," she continued.

"Here we go."

"What?"

Lucky folded his arms over his chest and steeled himself against those coaxing pewter gray eyes. "We country boys are familiar enough with manure to realize when we're knee-deep in the stuff. I figured there'd be a catch when you suddenly turned so agreeable. And sure enough, here it comes."

Jude's deep sigh caused her slender breasts to rise and fall beneath her pearl gray blouse. The blouse was silk; Lucky suspected that her perfumed skin would be even silkier. Not that he cared what Jude Lancaster's skin felt like, he assured himself. Then reluctantly realized that Kate wasn't the only liar in the O'Neill family.

"You're a very cynical man," she complained.

"Not cynical. Just a realist. Don't have much choice in the cow business. Now, admittedly we don't have a lot of high-rises in Cremation Creek. In fact, to be honest, I'd have to say that the movie theater is the tallest building in town. And my barn would probably come in second. But I do know enough about the fast lane to realize you didn't get that fancy corner office with all those windows by not being damn good at your job."

For some reason Jude heard herself opting for absolute honesty. "There are some in the city who might suggest I got that office because my father used to own the syndicate that publishes *Hunk of the Month*.'' Some people like Tycoon Mary, she thought but did not say.

He tilted his head, as if studying her from a new angle. "That may have helped in the beginning. But it wouldn't have been enough to keep you there," he decided. "So, it only makes sense that you wouldn't stop trying to talk me into posing for your magazine without giving it your best shot." Along with guts, determination was another thing Lucky could appreciate.

"I am good at what I do." Her voice, which had started out coaxingly warm, turned as chilly as the ice on a stock pond in February. "Which is why, even if I were to be fired, I could get another job anywhere in the publishing business. Like that." She snapped her unadorned fingers.

Aw, hell. She was arrogant to boot. And downright nervy for a half-pint female who didn't appear to have an ounce of surplus meat on her slender bones and barely reached his shoulder. Lucky had never been attracted to timid women. As he found himself once again wishing for a convenient hayloft, the ridiculousness of their situation had him feeling aggravated, aroused and reluctantly amused all at the same time.

"You're probably a crackerjack managing editor."

Jude's eyes narrowed, suggesting that she suspected a joke at her expense. "I am. However, I'm afraid Kate doesn't have the experience, or the reputation, to survive a shake-up as easily."

Lucky reluctantly put aside another enticing mental image of Jude, clad in a scrap of frothy lace, lying on a bed of sun-dappled straw. "Kate might lose her job?"

Lucky remembered how excited his sister had been when she'd called the ranch with the news that she'd won the competitive position which, from what he and Buck could tell in the early days, consisted mainly of fetching coffee and running the copy machine. It also hadn't paid enough to keep a hamster alive, which was why both men reluctantly accepted her decision to move in with Jack Peterson.

"She's my assistant. If I blow this issue, the publisher will replace me with her nephew—who's bound to bring in his girlfriend, the same bimbo he's installed as his secretary in marketing."

"And Kate would be out the door?"

"Before you could say 'Get along little dogie.'"

Lucky gave her a long look, trying to see if this was just another scam. After all, as Buck was always saying, baloney was still baloney, no matter how thin you sliced it.

"If you're lying—"

"Believe me, I'm not. Of course, it's always possible that Kate could survive and end up somewhere else at the magazine. Circulation, perhaps." Her tone suggested such an assignment to be the publishing world's equivalent of Boot Hill. "But the battle lines have already been drawn and although it's probably foolishly loyal of her, she's declared herself on my side."

"Katie was brought up to be loyal."

"Apparently loyalty—and responsibility—both run deep in the O'Neill family."

The observation didn't escape him. It had, of course, been made to remind him of his responsibility to his baby sister.

"You don't exactly fight fair, do you? Because that's definitely hitting below the belt."

"I have no idea what you mean."

She tossed her head in a way that caused another resurgence of the humor Lucky thought he'd left back home in Cremation Creek. He was half tempted to tell her that she was as cute as a newborn foal when she pulled out that princess-to-cowhand glare, and he figured she wouldn't really consider that much of a compliment.

"Well? Is it working?" she asked hopefully when he didn't answer right away.

"I don't know." Frustrated all over again, Lucky rubbed his unshaven chin. "I'll have to think on it."

"Fine. You'll have lots of time to ponder your sister's professional fate during our flight."

"Our flight? You're not coming to Wyoming."

"I've always wanted to see the Wild West. Especially since Kate's always describing it as Heaven on Earth. This is probably as good a time as any to see for myself if it lives up to your sister's billing."

He skimmed a look at the slim black purse and the briefcase she'd grabbed as she left the office. "I've heard of traveling light, but don't you think you're overdoing things?"

"I have a toothbrush in my purse. The laptop computer in my briefcase allows me to work anywhere. And I can buy essentials when I get to Wyoming. Besides, Kate's overnighting some casual clothes."

Lucky figured this woman's idea of casual would be more of those clingy silk blouses and designer jeans too tight to wear while climbing up on a horse. Not that it wouldn't be damn pleasant watching her try.

"You just don't give up, do you?"

"No. Not when it's something important. Something I care deeply about."

"No offense, Miz Lancaster—"

"Please call me Jude. As you said, there's probably not much need for formality in Cremation Creek."

She'd gotten that right. What Lucky was having trouble with was the idea of this chic New York woman in Cremation Creek in the first place.

"My point was, Jude," he said, earning a satisfied nod of her flaxen head, "I truly don't mean any disrespect, but as important as your magazine might be to you, it isn't on par with curing cancer or bringing about world peace."

If what he'd seen so far was any indication, he couldn't truthfully put it on par with *Hoof and Horns* magazine. But since he'd been brought up to be polite to women, Lucky decided there was no reason to mention that.

"We don't claim to be out to change the world," Jude said. "But *Hunk of the Month* does provide entertainment, which our subscription figures reveal must be fairly important to a number of people.

"And to be perfectly honest, I suppose, what I'm really concerned about is my reputation. And something else I can't really explain. But, for lack of another word, I'd have to call it pride. There are a lot of people relying on me. I don't want to let them down."

Pride was something else Lucky could identify with. For the first time he was beginning to get an inkling of why Katie considered her a close enough friend to lie for.

"You're not married." He took hold of the hand that had begun to nervously smooth nonexistent wrinkles from her skirt and stroked a fingertip over the fourth finger.

"No."

"Engaged?"

"No."

"Going steady?"

"No." Her voice wasn't as strong as it had been earlier. He touched a thumb to the inside of her wrist and felt her pulse hammer. *Interesting.*

"So, there's no one who's going to worry about you taking off to Wyoming with another man?"

"No one special."

"I guess your work gets in the way of a relationship."

"It takes up a lot of time."

"Must be rough, spending all those hours with near-naked men," he said dryly. He was still having trouble getting past that one.

The hand in his suddenly went cold. "Are you accusing me of sexually harassing my models?"

"Hell, no. Except for telling me to strip so you could check me for tattoos, you've been a perfect lady." Sarcasm crept into his tone.

"My interest in you is strictly professional."

Her unprofessionally racing pulse said otherwise. "You were looking at me as if I were some Red Angus bull you were considering buying."

And that idea still irked, dammit. Even if he had been known to look at women in much the same way back in his younger days.

"I'm sorry if I made you feel uncomfortable. But it's my job." She tugged her hand free and he felt a momentary sense of loss. "And besides, I thought you'd been apprised of the situation."

Lucky still thought hers was a damn sorry job, but seeing no point in insulting her further, he decided to turn the subject back to the other thing that continued to bother him.

"Is it true what you said? About Kate losing her job?"

"Absolutely."

"Would that really be such a bad deal? Dillon's an awful little tyke. Perhaps it'd be better if Kate stayed home for a time with him."

"I should have known you'd be a chauvinist."

"That's me," he agreed, refusing to rise to the bait. There was no way in hell he was going to apologize for caring about his sister and nephew.

"If I had my way, every female in the country would be barefoot and pregnant, only speak when spoken to and have her husband's supper on the table every night as soon he came home from the bar where he'd spent the day belching, telling dirty jokes about women's body parts, playing pool, drinking beer, spitting tobacco and doing all that other macho guy stuff females hate."

"You don't have to be so sarcastic."

"And a supposedly intelligent lady like you shouldn't be so quick to jump to conclusions," he countered. "I don't know what kind of home you grew up in, but the O'Neill women have always been equal partners in their marriages.

"Hollywood may focus on the cowboys and outlaws, but the simple fact is that if it hadn't been for those gutsy females who were willing to risk everything comfortable, everything they'd ever known, to make a new home for their husbands and children, well, hell, the U.S. border would probably still stop at the eastern banks of the Mississippi.

"And, in case you didn't know it, Wyoming's the Equality State because we were the first ones to give women the vote. My great-granddaddy just happened to be in the state legislature at the time," he added. "We've always been real proud of him for that vote."

"Well." Jude stared up at him. Those were the most words he'd strung together since he'd sauntered into her office on his wedge-heeled boots. She'd assumed that Lucky O'Neill was a stereotypical, laconic cowboy. But obviously, when he felt strongly about something, he didn't hesitate to state his opinion.

"That's a very impressive speech." It would also add a nice touch to the article, she thought, hoping that she could remember it long enough to write it all down.

"For a cowboy, you mean," he said mildly. "And it wasn't meant to be a speech. I was just trying to explain that you're wrong. I've nothing against women working. I watched my grandmother and mother work right alongside their husbands all of their lives.

"In fact, mom still travels most of the year with my dad, supplying stock to rodeos. I was just thinking that Kate might enjoy some time at home with her son."

"You might be right," Jude admitted. "But she doesn't really have a choice. Since they need the money."

"Jack's rich. I'll bet he pays more for dry-cleaning those fancy Italian suits than the ranch earned last quarter."

"He does all right, but it costs a lot more to live in New York than Wyoming."

"Then perhaps he ought to consider leaving New York," Lucky muttered.

Jude didn't respond to what she suspected was a rhetorical statement. There was no point in insulting his home state by mentioning that there undoubtedly wasn't much need for investment bankers in Wyoming. "Their biggest problem is that a great deal of what he earns goes to support his parents."

"His parents?" Lucky thought back to the attractive, well-dressed couple he'd met at Kate's wedding. Alicia and John Peterson had sported country club tans and smelled of old money. Lots of it.

Jude sighed and skimmed her fingers through the sleek slide of pale blond hair again. Her hands, he'd noticed, were like the rest of her—seldom still. "You don't know?"

"Apparently not."

She crossed her legs with a swish of silk on silk in a way that had Lucky's attention momentarily wandering off in a lustful direction again as he found himself wondering what she might be wearing beneath that short gray skirt.

Having grown up in a land that could be turned white by a summer blizzard, or golden brown by a scorching July sun, Lucky had learned to appreciate contrasts wherever he found them. And right now he was finding the contrast between that brief tight skirt and the trim little gray silk blouse buttoned all the way up to her slender neck more than a little appealing.

She caught his look and amazed him by blushing. "We were talking about Kate," she reminded him as she tugged ineffectually on the skirt.

"If you want to keep a man's mind on the conversation, darlin', you probably shouldn't wear something designed to make him want to take a bite out of your thigh."

The color in her cheeks deepened but the heat in her eyes, heat that this time seemed to have nothing to do with anger, made him believe he wasn't the only one suffering these unexpected, unruly feelings of lust.

"You want to bite my thigh?"

"Not hard," he assured her, worried she might think him some sort of dangerous pervert. "Just a few well-placed nibbles."

Another flare of estrogen shot through her like a hot flash. "Is every man in Mon—" Jude caught herself, "—Wyoming so direct?" Surprising Lucky, who wouldn't have believed a city woman still knew how to blush, the rosy color had reached the roots of her hair.

"I don't know about every man. But I've never been one to waste words."

He could have been a young Clint Eastwood come to life. Or Gary Cooper, with a touch of Jimmy Stewart's Destry thrown in. Jude decided that in the event she might ultimately leave *Hunk of the Month* magazine, she definitely wanted to go out with a bang. And Lucky O'Neill was pure TNT.

Every man has his price, Jude. She could practically hear her father reminding her yet again.

"Did I mention what we pay our hunks?"

Lucky actually cringed at the word. "I don't believe it came up. And it doesn't matter because—"

"Why don't you wait to hear me out before you make that stand?" she suggested sweetly. Then, although she'd briefly considered paying him less, since he was, after all, merely an amateur, she offered him precisely what she'd been willing to pay the superstud model Harper Stone.

4

"LADY, you've got to be joking!"

For the first time since he'd walked into her office, Jude felt as if she'd managed to gain the upper hand. He was more than surprised, she realized, looking at his dropped jaw. He was stunned.

"If there's one thing I never joke about, Mr. O'Neill, it's money." Actually, she'd never been one to tell many jokes, period, but that was beside the point.

"A guy can actually make that much just taking off his clothes for some magazine?"

"Not just *any* guy. And not just for *any* magazine. But I told you, we have a huge circulation that is growing every day—"

"Yeah, you've gone international."

He frowned, wondering if she had any way of knowing that what she was offering would cover the ranch operating expenses for the next six months and let him pay off the mortgage he'd had to take out on the house to make up for last fall's plummeting beef prices. He and Buck had argued about that, but he'd had no choice. Not if he wanted to keep the Double Ought in the family.

His father, who'd handed over the day-to-day running of the ranch to Lucky, had backed his son, but there'd been some hard words spoken and some uncomfortably silent breakfasts before the old man had finally given up his pique.

"I'll make you a deal," Jude offered, pressing her advantage. "As I said, we have high expectations for this issue. And now, having seen you, in the flesh, so to speak, I'm willing to bet that with you as our centerfold hunk, we'll sell out the minute the copies hit the streets.

"So, if we top last year's construction worker issue by ten percent, I'll pay you a bonus of an additional ten percent over what I'm already offering."

Jude knew it was risky. If Tycoon Mary didn't approve the increased payment, she could end up dipping into her trust fund. Perhaps it was merely a side effect of estrogen poisoning, but she was suddenly feeling recklessly like an old riverboat gambler.

He rubbed his square jaw again and gave her a long look. "There's something I still don't get."

Jude took encouragement in the fact that he hadn't rejected her new offer out of hand. "What's that?"

"I don't understand why women would want to look at pictures of naked men in the first place."

"I suppose you've never glanced through a *Playboy* or *Penthouse*?"

"That's different." Lucky wasn't exactly certain why. But it just wasn't the same thing, dammit. "I always thought women liked guys to be...well, guys."

"Women can appreciate all types of men." She felt obliged to defend her gender. "However, I suppose it's true that the readers who subscribe to *Hunk of the Month* are looking for a certain basic standard of masculinity. A man's man, so to speak." Which is why each of the ongoing "Working Man Blues" series had outsold the previous one.

In fact, just last month the ridiculously expensive—

and, in Jude's mind, redundant—focus groups Tycoon Mary had insisted on had revealed that issues featuring construction workers, cops or firemen flew off newsstands a lot faster than stockbrokers or bankers. Something Jude had figured out years ago. Which was yet another reason why she'd fought to use a real cowboy instead of a pretend one.

"Well, see now, that's precisely my point," Lucky argued stubbornly. "If a guy is getting paid to take his clothes off in front of a camera, he suddenly stops being a fireman or a cop. He's a model. A *male* model."

"Contrary to popular belief, male models aren't necessarily gay."

"I didn't say they were." Lucky swore, uncomfortable with this entire conversation. "It just seems, well..." He took off his hat and plowed his hands through thick chestnut hair that had been streaked silver and gold by the western sun. "It seems like kind of a sissy way to make a living."

She laughed at that and felt her tension begin to dissolve. "Believe me, there's not a woman in the entire world who could ever think of you as a sissy."

As the cab pulled up outside the terminal, Jude, who was watching him closely, saw the flicker of reluctant interest in his eyes and decided it was time to go in for the kill.

"I can certainly understand how a man of your conservative background might have some misgivings about being featured in a magazine like *Hunk of the Month*—"

"That's putting it mildly."

"I can also understand that you'd have pride—and rightfully so—in the cowboy image. I'm not just offering money, Lucky. I'm offering you the opportunity to promote that unique, larger-than-life western image to the world."

He shook his head and chuckled at that. "You know, Miss Lancaster, I think you were born in the wrong time. Because you definitely missed your calling."

"Oh?" She followed him out of the cab with another flash of thigh that made Lucky's mouth go as dry as high prairie dust.

When she caught him looking at her legs again, she wondered if he was going to suggest that she would have made a good dance hall girl. Or, perhaps, a female outlaw. Like Belle Starr. Jude, who'd never experienced a single rebellious moment in her life, found herself enjoying that idea.

He hooked his thumbs in his tooled leather belt and shifted his weight easily—arrogantly, she thought—onto one hip as he studied her. His next words punctured her pretty little mental balloon.

"You would have made one dynamite snake oil saleslady."

Irritation soared into the stratosphere. No one in her world—not even Tycoon Mary—would dare speak to her that way! Determined not to let him know he was getting to her, Jude managed, just barely, not to grind her teeth.

"If you're attempting to insult me, hoping that I'll take back my offer and walk away in a huff, it's not going to work. Publishing is a tough business and I've had to develop a thick skin. Besides—" she flashed him her most controlled, most insincere smile "—I just happen to have an entire arsenal of arguments I haven't used yet."

That stated, she turned and began walking toward the terminal. Not knowing whether to curse or laugh, but thoroughly enjoying the sway of her hips in that short skirt, Lucky set off after her.

There was another brief argument over seating when he discovered she'd arbitrarily arranged to have him moved to first class. Lucky wasn't about to be the first O'Neill in history to allow a female to pay his way. Apparently deciding to save her ammunition for more important battles, Jude opted to retreat from that little skirmish.

Unfortunately, the blue curtain separating them proved a damn flimsy barrier. In the same way her scent seemed to have slipped beneath his skin, thoughts of her had crept into his mind like a damn rustler sneaking through the night. He'd become all too aware that in her own way, Jude Lancaster could end up being as dangerous as Bodacious, the most dreaded rodeo bull alive, and the one that was responsible for breaking three of Lucky's ribs, his shoulder and his nose on two separate occasions back when he'd been foolish enough to believe that he could pick up some extra operating funds bull riding.

The money she was offering was admittedly appealing. And it wasn't as if he couldn't use it. But then again, it was looking to be a good year and Lucky wasn't any more in debt than most ranchers before fall roundup and he sure had been in worse straits. And survived. In fact, even without the magazine money, it was looking as if by the time his taxes were due next March—for some reason that had never seemed fair, ranchers had to file a month ahead of the rest of the country—he'd end up in the black, even after paying off those bankers Buck was all the time bitching about.

No, if it was just the money, he'd pass on the entire cockeyed scheme without a second thought.

But the idea of Kate losing her job grated. The idea of her actually needing the money was cause for both irritation and concern. At least, despite all his earlier misgivings about Jack Peterson, Lucky had assumed he'd be able to support Kate and Dillon. The problem was, as much as part of him wanted to turn around and go back and punch his brother-in-law out again for complicating matters, another part—the part that had been brought up to respect his elders—couldn't fault the guy for taking care of his parents. Lord knows, there wasn't anything he wouldn't do for his parents. Or for Buck.

Maybe he could use any money left after paying off the mortgage to set up some sort of college savings account for Dillon. Although he was typically a lot more concerned with cattle futures than Wall Street, Lucky knew that these stock market bull years were causing money to grow by leaps and bounds. The problem was, in order to get the money, he'd have to take his clothes off for millions of women all over the world.

Of course, it wasn't exactly as if they'd be in the room with him, Lucky reminded himself. The only person who'd get to see him in the altogether would be that photographer who'd shown up just before the plane took off, who was, thankfully, a man, since there was no way he'd consider letting some female photographer take pictures of him in little more than his birthday suit. It'd probably be like the locker room at high school. Except, of course, nobody had taken pictures of his naked butt back when he'd been snapping towels after basketball practice.

Lucky dragged his hands down his face and wished that life was as simple as it had been portrayed in those old John Wayne westerns Buck was always watching on TV through that fancy new satellite dish.

By THE TIME the plane finally began its descent into Cheyenne, Jude, who felt as if she'd been traveling for days, had new appreciation for all those stalwart women who'd climbed up onto buckboards and covered wagons and headed west with their husbands to carve out a new life. And they hadn't even had a movie to watch while en route.

She looked out the window as the brown, wide-open land loomed closer. It looked so large. So empty. So lonely. Then she viewed a familiar green sight that flowed over the landscape like an emerald river.

"There's a golf course," she murmured to her seatmate, Zach Newman, the photographer who'd managed to reach the gate just before takeoff.

He glanced up from the latest issue of *Outdoor Photography* magazine. "I didn't realize you played golf."

"I don't."

She preferred tennis. Partly because it avoided direct competition with her golfer father and partly because its faster pace suited her better than a grindingly slow game that seemed to take all day to complete.

She'd also taken horseback riding lessons and enjoyed them immensely. And had made a stab at piano lessons only to quickly discover that she hadn't an iota of talent. But all those simple recreational pleasures seemed as if they'd occurred in another time. Another world. She couldn't remember when she'd last gone to the club. These past years, *Hunk of the Month* had taken over her life.

"A golf course is a good sign, don't you think?" she asked, dragging her mind away from the surprisingly depressing thoughts concerning her less-than-scintillating private life. "I mean, it makes everything seem more normal."

"More like home?"

"Exactly." She was relieved he understood.

She was also mistaken. He laughed at that, a rich, warm laugh that drew appreciative looks from the two first-class flight attendants who were polishing up the galley in preparation for landing.

"Only you would consider your high-powered, workaholic New York life-style normal."

It was not the first time he'd accused her of parochialism. Jude lifted her chin. "There's nothing wrong with work. And although people are always focusing on the negative aspects of New York, in many ways it's just another small town."

"Your little privileged East Side-Hamptons sphere of it, perhaps," he allowed. "But take it from a guy who grew up outside Laramie, sweetheart, you've never had a *normal* day in your life."

While she was trying to decide whether or not to take issue with the statement that sounded suspiciously like an insult, something else he'd said captured her attention.

"You grew up outside Laramie?" She skimmed a look over the man wearing the Manhattan uniform of black linen slacks, a black Calvin Klein T-shirt and loosely structured jacket. "Laramie, Wyoming?"

"It's the only Laramie I know of."

"But I don't understand." She studied him more closely, as if actually seeing him for the first time. "I'm certain I remember your résumé stating you come from Santa Barbara."

"That's true, so far as it goes. I studied photography

at the Brooks Institute there. The way I figure it, that's all that's relevant to my work. Why should it make a difference where I was born? Or where I attended third grade?"

"I suppose none," she admitted. "But I still can't understand why you felt the need to edit your biography."

"Can't you?"

There was a faint challenge in his voice. A harsher tone Jude had never heard before. "No," she insisted, holding her ground.

"It's all a matter of perception. Take our hunky cowboy back in coach." He jerked his dark head toward the blue curtain separating the cabins. "What's the first thing you thought when you saw him?"

"That he was the answer to my prayers."

"After that."

"That he was going to send sales figures through the roof."

"I'd say that's a given. You haven't had a hunk this good-looking since that Philadelphia pipe fitter."

Who had also been, Jude recalled, in a long-term relationship with a female impersonator who looked more like Diana Ross than the diva of Motown did herself.

"If you can get O'Neill to agree to pose, readers will undoubtedly find him about as intoxicating as a stiff shot of Wild Turkey," Zach said, bringing her thoughts back to the matter at hand. "What else did you think?"

"Nothing," she hedged.

Jude felt her newly discovered temper flare when he had the nerve to laugh again. "Liar. I'd bet my new macro lens that you felt the exact same instantaneous lust that hit me when I first came face-to-face with his sister."

"You and Kate?" Jude glanced at him in surprise. "I never knew."

It was his turn to look chagrined. "There isn't really anything to know. She was engaged to Peterson, and although I've never been all that wild about rules, poaching another guy's girl is one line I'd never cross."

"Okay, now I believe you're from Laramie." She folded her arms, tilted her head and shook her head in amusement. "That remark sounds amazingly like Lucky O'Neill's so-called Code of the West."

"Go ahead and scoff all you want, but the truth is that there *is* a code, of sorts. It's not like it's written down or anything—"

"I know. Lucky and I have been through that, too. A man just knows what's right and wrong. Then does what he has to do."

He shrugged. "That's about it. But you need to keep in mind that things are different out here. People don't respond to the same triggers that work in New York.

"I'll bet, when you and Kate came up with your cockeyed scheme to trick the guy into being your Hunk of the Month, you figured a simple cowboy from Cremation Creek, Wyoming, would be an easy sell."

"Well, perhaps I thought he'd be a bit more open-minded—"

"Malleable, you mean."

"Open-minded," she repeated firmly.

"Easy," he corrected mildly. "Which is why I tend not to broadcast where I'm from. People in our business only want to work with the big hitters. They want to feel they're paying for the best and the brightest. The most creative. And they're sure as hell not going to believe they can find that in a guy who grew up on a Wyoming ranch."

"You're probably right." Feeling a bit like Alice after she'd taken that dive down the rabbit hole, Jude decided this would undoubtedly go down as one of the strangest days of her life. "But there's still one little thing you're overlooking."

"What's that?"

"We're on this plane, about to land in Cheyenne. And O'Neill still hasn't said no."

"That's not what Kate said when she called me and told me to get my cameras out to the airport. She said he'd turned you down flat."

"He might have not found my first offer exactly to his liking—"

"Nor your second, I'll bet."

"We seem to have reached a bit of an impasse," she admitted reluctantly. "But my point is, that as soon as we land, I can take another shot at him."

"On his turf. Which effectively gives him control of the situation."

Good point. And one she was determined to ignore.

"Ah, ye of little faith," she said, patting his arm as she flashed him a quick, self-assured smile, not quite certain who she was trying to convince—Zach or herself. "The cowboy's too polite—and chauvinistic, which fortunately also translates to chivalrous—to leave me alone at the airport. Especially since I'm his baby sister's best friend. Which means he'll have no choice but to take us out to his Boot Hill ranch with him—"

"It's not Boot Hill. The O'Neill spread is called the Double Ought. It's located outside Cremation Creek."

She waved the correction away with her hand. The

diamond on her watch face flashed, reminding her yet again of the promotion she'd worked so hard to achieve. "Whatever. The bottom line is, one way or another, whatever I have to do, I'm going to convince that hunk of a cowboy to sign on the dotted line."

They were, admittedly, brave words. As the wheels of the jet touched down, Jude only hoped she could live up to them.

5

IT DEFINITELY WASN'T EASY keeping up with Lucky's long-legged stride as they made their way through the terminal, passing the standard gates, bars, newsstands and a display of historic airport memorabilia that at any other time Jude might have enjoyed stopping to study. She was practically forced to run on the high heels that were horrendously impractical for work, but gave her a few important inches in height. But since she had a feeling that he was somehow testing her, she refused to give him the upper hand.

There was a short wait at the luggage carousel for Zach to retrieve his bags. Although he never let his camera and lenses out of sight while traveling, the two oversize metal boxes filled with tripods and lighting equipment were too large to be carried on.

Jude was looking around for a skycap when, without a word, Lucky simply lifted one of the boxes off the carousel, hefted it onto one shoulder as if it were a bale of hay, and began walking toward the terminal exit.

"Oh yes," Zach murmured to Jude as he grabbed the second box, "he'll definitely do."

"Lucky O'Neill will more than do. That cowboy's going to set the standard."

Even more reason, she considered, for resigning after this issue. It was, after all, always best to go out on top. *Cosmo* had been trying to recruit her for years.

Maybe when she returned to town, she'd call the managing editor and casually suggest lunch. Then, of course, there was *Vanity Fair*, which had also begun courting her. Going to work for the slick publication would also give her an opportunity to hang out with movie stars and politicians.

Remembering her father's edict about the importance of always moving forward, Jude decided to definitely give a great deal of thought to making a major change. Right after she saved this all-important issue.

Myriad sensations flooded over her as she walked out of the terminal. She was vividly aware of the pungent scent of evergreens, the endless vastness of the clear blue sky and most of all the heat that hit like a fist in the solar plexus.

"I thought Wyoming was cold." In her mind's eye she'd pictured postcard scenes of jagged, white-capped mountains and swirling blizzards. She also remembered long-time friends Chip and Sissy Cunningham waxing enthusiastic about a trip to Jackson Hole, where they'd been invited to a dinner with the President and First Lady.

"It gets chilly enough, in the winter. But this is summer."

Sweat popped out on her forehead like a sudden attack of the measles, her panty hose felt as if they were melting into her flesh and her high heels were sinking into the hot asphalt. The sun was blazing a brilliant yellow in a sky so blue it resembled a robin's egg. Jude squinted as she dug into her briefcase for her sunglasses.

"Thank you so very much for pointing that out to me." The heels of her Italian leather pumps made little sucking sounds as she struggled even harder to catch up with him. "At least we don't have to worry about you getting any vital parts frostbitten while we're photographing the layout."

Her jibe hit home, just as she'd intended. He paused, glancing back over his shoulder as he waited for her to catch up.

"I haven't agreed to be photographed for any layout," he reminded her. "As for vital parts, I seem to recall you promising that they'd stay covered."

"That's our editorial policy," she assured him yet again.

"That's good to hear. Although, if I do agree, I suppose it probably couldn't hurt to have you check me over for sunburn afterward. Just to make sure." Lines crinkled outward from his brown eyes as he flashed her a grin hotter and potentially more dangerous than the huge western sun beating down on them.

"I suppose I could do that." She pulled the glasses back off and aimed a cool glance at the vital parts in question. "Since I doubt it would take all that much time."

He laughed at that. A rich, appealing laugh that came from deep in his chest. "Damned if you don't have a smart mouth, Jude Lancaster." Reaching out the hand that wasn't holding on to the metal trunk, he skimmed a finger down her nose. "Makes a guy want to lock lips with you just to shut you up."

Irritated on principle, annoyed at that taunting male smile, and wary of the way his light touch once again lit internal sparklers, Jude slapped his hand away.

"Let's get one thing straight, cowboy. I'm admittedly willing to do just about whatever it takes to convince you to be my hunk. Including giving you a piece of the action." She tossed back her hair and lifted her chin. "But I draw the line at locking lips, or any other ideas along those lines you might have."

He cut a glance toward Zach who, laden down with camera equipment, was watching the exchange with obvious male amusement.

"Little lady's got a short fuse."

Zach had the discretion to cover up his chuckle with a cough. "Never known her to rile so easily," he said, dropping into a lazy, unfamiliar western drawl that caused Jude to glare at him. "You must bring out the worst in her, O'Neill."

"Yeah." Lucky tilted his hat back with his thumb. "Always did like a female with spunk, though." He tilted his head again, his brown eyes brightening like newly mined copper as he gave her another perusal. "She's a mite skinny—"

"It's a city thing." The photographer couldn't quite keep his lips from twitching. "The scrawnier the better, back east, it seems."

"Scrawny?" Jude's hands were at her hips, her eyes shooting flaming arrows at this colleague she'd come to think of as a friend.

"Well, no matter." Lucky ignored Jude's outburst as he continued the conversation with Zach. "Buck's cooking is bound to put some curves on her."

"I have curves!" Jude couldn't believe she'd just been put in the position of defending the body she'd worked like hell to tone and harden. "But that's irrelevant, since my body is absolutely none of your business."

"You didn't seem to have any problems with discussing my body. In detail," Lucky reminded her. "I was just returning the compliment."

"I merely, in a strictly professional manner, pointed

out your, uh, assets." Her eyes narrowed dangerously. "And perhaps we're using a different dictionary, but I've never considered *scrawny* to be a compliment."

"It was your friend here who used that word. Personally, although I usually tend to prefer a bit more meat on a lady's bones, there's no denying that what little you've got is definitely prime, darlin'."

His quick, cocky-as-hell grin caused a three-alarm fire to blaze upward from the collar of her blouse. Damn the man! She'd never blushed in her life! Why, until Lucky O'Neill had strode into her office, like a Brahma bull let loose in Tiffany's, she hadn't even been aware that she could blush.

"This is a ridiculous conversation." She let out a frustrated breath and jammed her sunglasses back onto her warm face. "If you don't mind, I'd like to get to Cremation Creek before I melt into the pavement. I still have to check into a hotel—"

"Now that's going to be a bit hard to do," Lucky said.

"Oh?" She arched a brow in a challenging gesture learned from her father and folded her arms across the blouse that was beginning to stick to her damp body. Her damp, *scrawny* body. Whatever Lucky was driving, she desperately hoped it had air-conditioning. "And why is that?"

"Because there aren't any hotels in Cremation Creek. Or any of the high-fashion boutiques or fancy beauty salons you're undoubtedly used to. In fact, there aren't even any supermarkets. Just Johnny Murphy's Feed and Fuel. And market. And chain-saw art gallery," he added as an afterthought.

"Isn't that droll," she muttered, not even wanting to guess at the artistic quality of chain-saw art. "And I find it difficult to believe that even out here in the middle of nowhere, it's possible for a town to have only one building. You wouldn't be pulling the scrawny city slicker's leg now, would you, Mr. O'Neill?"

"I thought we'd already determined that I'd rather bite it, Miz Lancaster." His answer drew another smothered cough from Zach. "But I doubt if I'm alone in that idea since I saw more than one man walk into the wall when you sashayed through the terminal in that short tight skirt."

"Now you're accusing me of wearing my skirt too tight?"

"Darlin', there is no such thing as a skirt being too tight," Lucky responded with easy humor. Lord help him, he really was starting to enjoy the woman. Which was, he feared, even more dangerous than merely lusting after her.

"The point I was making was that skirt—and the sexy lady wearing it—would make any healthy man's mind start painting pictures."

"Dirty pictures."

"Erotic pictures," he corrected easily. "Even a dumb wrangler like me knows the difference."

She gave him a long, probing look. "I don't believe you're dumb at all. In fact, I think your aw-shucks, Roy Rogers cowboy act is exactly that. An act you pull out whenever it suits you. Such as when you want to put people off guard in a negotiating situation." Jude decided that her father, who'd always prided himself on his negotiation skills, would have appreciated Lucky O'Neill's unorthodox tactics.

"Now that's a right interesting idea," he drawled. "I'll have to think on it. After we get you settled in at the Double Ought." He turned and started walking toward a fire-engine red pickup.

"Surely there's somewhere else to stay other than your ranch?" This time he wasn't even attempting to hold back his stride. Lifting her skirt even higher, wishing she'd worn slacks to the office today, she took off after him again.

"Sure." He stopped in front of the huge red truck boasting four tires in the rear, two in front, and a roomy back seat with its own door. A metal rendition of a ram's head adorned the wide hood in what she took to be a macho version of the Jaguar her father had always kept garaged at their summer home in the Hamptons. "You're more than welcome to stay in the bunkhouse with the hands."

He tossed the trunk in the back and opened the doors with a click of the remote on his key chain. "I can't guarantee much privacy, but you'll undoubtedly be the most popular roommate any of those horny wranglers have ever had."

Her heart sunk right down to the toes of the impractical high heels she'd had the misfortune to wear today. "There really isn't a hotel or motel in town?"

"I already told you—"

"I know. The Feed and Fuel. And market." Her frustrated sigh ruffled the blond hair that the high country breeze was blowing across her brow. "And chain-saw art gallery." Her sarcastic tone revealed what she thought of that last item.

"Don't knock it until you've seen it," he advised. "Clint McLaury creates the best grizzly holding a fish of any carver in the state. Johnny sells so many out of the store that Clint's had to give up cowboying to keep up with demand.

"Johnny also runs the movie theater on the weekends," Lucky revealed while Jude was still trying to decide if he was actually serious about the chain-saw grizzly bear art. "It was built as an opera house back in the early part of the century. The mayor—that'd be my great-granddaddy Virgil—had been lobbying for the railroad to come through and he wanted to be ready to invite Lillie Langtry to perform in Cremation Creek.

"Unfortunately, the politicians in Laramie pulled more weight, and old Virgil never did get his railroad. And Lillie never came. But the entire fiasco did leave us with a mighty fine theater."

This had to be "The Twilight Zone." Jude stared up at him, momentarily speechless, positive he was teasing her again, equally afraid he just might not be.

"Surely there's another town—"

"Not within fifty miles. Which would make your daily commute back and forth to the ranch a bit of a long haul. Especially during afternoon thunderstorms."

She'd seen a television movie of the week about a family getting washed away in a flash flood somewhere in the remote west. Wyoming? Montana? Arizona? Whatever. The idea was definitely less than appealing.

It was when she finally decided to concentrate on what Lucky *wasn't* saying, instead of what he was, that Jude felt a renewed burst of optimism. She could survive this, she assured herself.

"You wouldn't be inviting us to stay at your ranch if you hadn't decided to pose for us." He would have just left Zach and her at the airport to catch the next plane back to New York.

"I told you, I haven't made up my mind." Knowing

that there was no way she was going to be able to climb up into the seat in that skirt and those spindly little shoes without some help, Lucky put his hands on her waist and lifted her with ease. "I want to make certain that when I do, I've considered all the options. I've always believed that when a cowboy climbs into a saddle, he'd better be prepared to ride."

Jude assured herself that it was only the stress of the day, uncharacteristic jet lag, and the disorienting feeling of finding herself in such an alien place that had her imagining she could feel the imprint of each of his fingers through her blouse. Hear the scrape of rough calluses against the silk.

"I think the heat must be melting my brain," she muttered when he joined her in the cab of the truck, leaving the back seat to Zach. "Because I almost understand that one."

He slanted her a lazy look as he twisted the key in the ignition, bringing the huge truck to life. Air even hotter than outside the cab began blasting from the dashboard, ruffling her hair, feeling like a desert sirocco against her face. His lips tilted in a devilish grin that she imagined most women—women not nearly as focused and controlled as she—would find impossible to resist. His eyes, as they skimmed over her face, which she feared was undoubtedly dripping makeup, had turned that warm copper hue again.

"Now you're getting it." He reached out a large dark hand, ruffling her hair in an almost fraternal gesture. "We'll make a cowgirl out of you yet, New York."

She folded her arms and turned to look straight out the windshield. "I wouldn't bet the ranch on that, cowboy."

He chuckled as he pulled out of the parking lot.

"You've definitely got spunk. Buck's flat-out goin' to love you."

"That would be your grandfather. The Wyoming Will Rogers."

"Now there you go, bein' sarcastic again, but the fact of the matter is that Buck'd probably enjoy that description."

"I assume he's a cowboy, too?"

"Used to be. These days he's kind of chief cook and bottle washer. But in his time, there wasn't a better cowpuncher than Buck O'Neill."

The honest affection in his voice reminded Jude of how she'd come to be here in Wyoming in the first place. If Lucky hadn't been the type of man to value family, he never would have rushed off to New York to rescue his sister. He might be chauvinistic and frustratingly brash, but there was no denying that deep down inside, he was the kind of man who deserved his sister's admiration.

"Dammit, O'Neill, after all the grief you've put me through these past hours, I'd just about made up my mind not to like you."

He laughed at her muttered words. "Now that's undoubtedly the first totally truthful statement you've made since I walked into your fancy white office." He slanted her a friendly look. "And I've gotta admit, New York, you're startin' to kinda grow on me, too."

Once again, Jude uncharacteristically allowed hope's sweet song to sing in her veins. "Enough that you'd agree to be my hunk?"

"You just don't give up, do you?"

She thought she heard a grudging respect in his tone and decided that since Lucky was obviously the kind of man to appreciate honesty, it could only help her cause if she told him the absolute truth.

"Not when it's something that matters a lot to me."

"Like your magazine."

"No. Well, of course I feel strongly about *Hunk of the Month*. But it's more my reputation I'm thinking about. And living up to expectations."

"Since your daddy owned your magazine, I suppose we're talking about his expectations. "

It was not a question, but Jude answered him anyway. "Yes."

Silence settled over the cab of the truck as Lucky mulled that one over. He was definitely a man comfortable with lengthy conversational gaps. Which made sense, Jude decided, since although she didn't have the faintest idea what a cowboy really did on a day-to-day basis, she suspected he'd spend a great deal of time alone out in the pastures. Or the range, or whatever they called it. She also strongly doubted that cows would make scintillating conversationalists.

Just when she'd begun to wonder if he'd forgotten they'd been having a conversation of sorts, he finally responded.

"Trying to live up to someone else's expectations is a lot like wearing another man's hat or riding his horse. With a few concessions, you can make it work, but neither one will ever fit like those you break in yourself." His tone was serious. Thoughtful.

"You sound as if you might know something about that."

"Some people around here still call my dad—who's in his fifties, by the way—*Buck's Boy*. Part of the reason Dad took up working as a rodeo stock supplier was he knew he'd never live up to my granddaddy's rodeo

fame. And to hear Buck tell it, he took up rodeoing because he didn't have my great-granddaddy's knack for
gentling horses. And none of us have Virgil's skill at
politics...

"I suppose it's inevitable, when your family roots go
deep in a place, that folks are going to make compari-
sons. Some people choose to leave, to start someplace
fresh on their own, where they can be judged by their
own standards.

"But if you're one of those who decides to stay, the
trick is to figure out your own individual role in the
scheme of things. And just try to do your best in that
arena."

"So, what's your particular talent?" Jude realized
she was genuinely curious as to what made this seemingly laconic man tick. "Your role in the O'Neill
arena?"

"You know, I've pondered on that a lot myself
lately." Lucky rubbed his jaw. "I've got a knack with
horses, but nothing like my great-granddaddy's reputation. And I sure don't like traveling, so there's no
way I'd be happy being a rodeo stock man. And I figure, with my habit of speaking my mind straight out,
I'd last about ten minutes in politics. And, although I'll
do a little bronc busting from time to time to see if I can
pick up some quick operating funds for the ranch, I'm
probably a worse rodeo rider than my dad."

"I think you're being overly modest there," Jude argued. "Since your buckle says you're a champion."

Although the conversation had turned almost serious, Lucky grinned at that. "You noticed."

"It's part of my job to notice everything about you,"
she reminded him.

"That's some kind of job you've got, looking at half-dressed men all day."

"There happens to be a great deal more to *Hunk of the Month* than just beefcake."

"Yeah, I'll bet all those subscribers read it for the articles," he drawled wickedly.

Not wanting to get drawn into an argument when she still didn't have his name on the dotted line of a contract, Jude refused to rise to the accusation. "I believe we were discussing your work," she reminded him. "And what you do best."

"Well, now, not that I'd be one to brag about myself or anything, but I've been told that pleasuring pretty women is one of my better talents."

"You are, without a doubt, the most amazingly arrogant man I've ever met."

The maddening grin didn't fade from his face. "It's only arrogance if it's not true. And it's only braggin' if you haven't done it. If you want, I'd be more than happy to demonstrate—"

"I told you, my interest in you is purely professional." She folded her arms.

"Yeah, I know…you're just interested in my body."

There was no way she was going to touch that line. "You truly are impossible."

"So some people say," he agreed on a soft, rumbling chuckle. "I don't suppose a smart city girl would be willing to take a little advice?"

She didn't answer. But her shrug was a go-ahead gesture.

"When you're trying to get a man to do something he really doesn't want to do, you'll have a lot better luck if you work him like you would your best cutting horse."

"I've never owned a cutting horse."

"Well, if you had, you'd have figured out that it's always best to take it slow, take it easy. And, most importantly, don't rush him."

"I'll keep that in mind."

He nodded, seemingly satisfied. "Why don't you do that?"

This time his mild tone didn't fool her for a second. It was a warning, pure and simple. One that, if she wanted to come out the winner in this ongoing test of wills, she'd be wise to heed.

6

THEY PASSED THROUGH Cremation Creek on the way to the Double Ought, confirming Lucky's allegation that Jude wouldn't find anyplace to stay in the town—not that two structures could actually qualify as a full-fledged town, she thought. The movie theater was a grand two-and-a-half-story frame structure with old-fashioned round lightbulbs surrounding a marquee announcing an upcoming three-day Clint Eastwood festival.

"The Gilded Lily?" Jude murmured as she read the name painted in gleaming gold across the arched facade of the theater.

"Virgil thought if he named it that, Lillie Langtry'd be more likely to come. I'd have no way of knowing, but I'll wager there are various versions of that name all over the west. This was lonely country, and there weren't a lot of eligible women, so it probably wasn't surprising that she'd inspire a lot of male fantasies."

"I suppose you're right." Jude recalled the land they'd driven through on the way to the town and suspected that while many would still call it lonely, in a way she'd found it oddly peaceful.

He pulled into the huge parking lot across the street from The Gilded Lily, cutting the engine in front of the Feed and Fuel. The store had obviously expanded over the decades, ending up part gray stone, part log cabin, and part aluminum siding. An oversize American flag flying outside the door proudly proclaimed that this was also the home of the Cremation Creek United States Post Office.

While Lucky pumped fuel into the tank of the dually pickup, Jude took the opportunity to run inside the store to use the bathroom, which she was more than a little relieved to discover was spotless and smelled like a pine forest.

The inside of the general store was like nothing she'd ever seen. It was unbelievably small—only about a quarter of the size of the compact urban markets she was accustomed to—yet crammed to the rafters with so many items it reminded her of the inside of a Fabergé egg. But not from Sotheby.

Perhaps a merger of *Guns and Ammo* and Wal-Mart, she decided, cringing as she noticed the stuffed animals lining the tops of the food shelves laden down with every junk food known to man. The animals bore no resemblance to the fluffy blue and white bunny she'd bought for Dillon when he'd been born, but were the type that had once been alive and now seemed to stare down at her with their wide, unblinking, yellow marble eyes.

On the far wall, next to a rack of plastic animal calls—which, according to the hand-painted sign, were guaranteed to draw wild beasts as varied as elk and varmints—she could see a padlocked display case with guns and knives for sale. Several of the guns were replicas of Old West sidearms of the types Jesse James or Billy the Kid or Wyatt Earp might have favored.

In front of the case, near the counter, was the most amazing item in the store. The chain-saw art.

The featured piece was tall—towering above her

head—and depicted, exactly as Lucky had described, a bear holding a fish. The work, while crudely primitive, was strangely powerful. As was the amazingly exorbitant price, which also backed up Lucky's assertion that the artist, Clint McLaury, was extremely popular.

It crossed Jude's mind that she should question Lucky about McLaury, and if he was even reasonably attractive, perhaps she could use him in a future issue of the magazine. Not as a featured centerfold—although it might be an unfair stereotype, artistic hunks did not sell magazines—but as one of the "Real Guys We Love to Look At" filler pieces. A hunk with a chain saw would undoubtedly appeal to that same audience that had made the blue-collar issues such a success.

She bought a Hershey's bar and a Coke from a thirty-something woman with long auburn corkscrew curls and a lush *Sports Illustrated* cover girl body Jude suspected Lucky would definitely appreciate. That thought brought up another: Cremation Creek was obviously a small community, which meant that Lucky undoubtedly knew the woman.

Had he ever dated her? Danced cheek to cheek at the local saloon, perhaps, while the jukebox twanged out a country-and-western tune about fickle women and faithless cowboys? Had they made out in the balcony of that movie theater that had been built in hopes of luring Lillie Langtry to Cremation Creek? Had he slept with her?

When she felt a twinge of something that felt too much like jealousy, Jude shook it off before she could think about it too deeply. She remembered to smile and thank the woman who told her, with a perky smile and obvious curiosity, to have a nice day. Jude noticed she put her money into an old-fashioned cigar box that apparently served as a cash register.

"Well?" Lucky asked as she rejoined the two men. His eyes were literally dancing with anticipation as he waited to hear her reaction.

"I never realized they made so many kinds of cheese puffs," she said as he gave her another boost up onto the high seat. "And the natives seem friendly."

"Dixie's always been a sweetheart. We had ourselves a lot of fun back in high school." His easy words caused the green-eyed monster living inside her to stir again. "And Lila's just as nice."

"Lila?"

"Her twin sister."

There were two of them? Terrific. Jude slouched down in the seat, unwrapped the candy bar and assured herself that she didn't care who Lucky O'Neill had slept with.

JUDE HADN'T REALLY given any thought to the O'Neill ranch house. If asked, she supposed she would have expected something rustic, created of hand-hewn logs, perhaps. Something the Cartwright boys would have felt at home in.

That being the case, the white clapboard two-story house with forest green shutters and a wide, screened-in porch that seemed to run around all four sides, came as a distinct surprise. Although, with occasional trips to Chicago, she'd only ever flown over the Midwest, she suspected Lucky's house would have fit in just fine at the edge of an Iowa cornfield.

"It's lovely," she murmured, gazing out beyond the house to the acres of grass and gold hay. "Homey."

If she'd gone into advertising instead of publishing,

this was just the kind of house she'd want to use for a soup commercial. Or a Hallmark home-for-the-holidays special.

"It's a money pit," Lucky said. "Every time we turn around something's gotta be fixed or replaced. But you're right about one thing. Seventy-five years of O'Neills living here have definitely made it a home."

"Got yourself some good pastureland, too," Zach noted.

"We had a lot of early summer showers, so the grass is staying green longer. And for the most part the grasshoppers have left us alone this summer. Unlike last year when they just about wiped us out."

"I remember when I was a kid, about sixteen or seventeen, we were hit with them real bad," Zach said. "Damn things nearly put us out of the ranching business."

"Surely you're not serious," Jude said, looking back out at what looked like an endless sea of green. Certainly mere insects couldn't do so much damage?

"You grew up on a ranch?" Lucky asked at the same time.

Zach answered Jude's question first. "Didn't you ever read *Little House on the Prairie* when you were a girl?"

"I don't think so." She decided not to mention that her father, on the rare occasion that he'd tolerated fiction, had insisted upon the classics by such authors as Dickens or Jonathan Swift.

"Well, if you had, you'd know those gluttonous devils can wipe out a year's worth of grain in an afternoon. It is not," he said dryly, "a pretty sight." He turned toward Lucky. "My family's got a place in the Snowy Range area."

"Nice country," Lucky said as he pulled up in front of the house. "I knew a Kayla Newman who was from that part of the country, I don't suppose—"

"Kayla's my little sister," Zach said. "My folks died in a car accident up around Jackson Hole a couple winters ago, so now she's running the ranch with her husband, who used to be a foreman on a place up in Montana. They have two kids and a third on the way."

"I remember Kayla bein' a real pretty gal. And smart as a whip." Lucky said. "And wasn't she also a pretty good barrel racer?"

"State champ three years running," Zach said with obvious brotherly pride.

Lucky gave a nod of approval. "It's good you were able to keep the place in the family. Lots of folks around here have been losing their ranches to developers or big conglomerates."

"I would have come home from New York before I'd have let that happen."

Zach's quiet, yet determined tone made Jude realize yet again that he was obviously not exactly what—or who—he appeared to be at first glance.

Lucky nodded again and Jude took his grunt for grudging approval. She wondered if perhaps, since they obviously had so much in common, Zach might be able to succeed where she'd failed in convincing Lucky to cooperate.

"Don't even think it," the photographer murmured into her ear as Lucky went to retrieve the trunks from the back of the truck.

"Think what?" she asked with feigned innocence.

"I saw that look flash in your scheming silver eyes. That let's-make-a-deal look you get when you're plotting something out. I've liked working with you, Jude.

A lot. You're sharp as barbwire, efficient as all get out, you're great to look at and you smell real good, too.

"But I'm not real convinced this is the best thing for O'Neill to do."

"Isn't that for him to decide?"

"Of course. But I could tell by the gleam in your eyes that you were thinking of enlisting me in your campaign to get the guy to pose. And even if I didn't have my personal doubts about the wisdom of this idea, nothing I could say would change his mind."

"You sound awfully certain of that." Jude had gotten the same impression, but had been hoping she might be wrong.

"Honey, I know guys like O'Neill. I grew up with them. Hell, I used to *be* one. Believe me, it'd be easier to turn a steer back into a bull than make your potential hunk go against his own personal code."

As Zach went to help Lucky with the camera equipment, Jude decided that she was really beginning to hate the Code of the West.

Although she was certain he wouldn't appreciate the comparison, Buck O'Neill reminded Jude a little bit of Gabby Hayes. He was a short, spry man, lean as a whip and, despite his age, looked as hard as the huge granite boulders they'd passed on the drive from Cheyenne.

A lifetime working outdoors had weathered his face to the hue of a hazelnut, an iron gray mustache fringed his top lip, and his eyes, as they skimmed over her, were as bright as the sky overhead. She also suspected, from the appraisal in his gaze, that the man was sizing her up and not particularly approving of what he found.

Tough.

"Hello, Mr. O'Neill." She held out her hand and

gave him a friendly smile meant to charm. From the way Lucky had spoken of his grandfather, she assumed he respected the older man's opinion a great deal. Which meant that she'd best get Buck on her side as soon as possible. "My name is Jude Lancaster. I work with your granddaughter in New York and have heard a great deal about you."

"From Katie?" he asked.

"No. Kate and I mostly talk about work when we're at the office. But your grandson certainly quotes you a great deal."

"He does, does he?"

"He certainly does. Why, he made you out to be a modern-day Mark Twain or Will Rogers. In fact, I was thinking that we should interject some of your pearls of western wisdom into the article."

"Article?"

She'd succeeded in getting his attention. "Kate didn't explain when you spoke with her?"

"Said Dillon was fussing," he grumbled. A guarded look came across his face as he studied her the way he might study a man sitting across the table holding a card hand close to his chest. "Didn't have any time to get into details. The gal just wanted me to know that Lucky was bringing company."

"I see. Well, I'm managing editor of the magazine we both work for and I was hoping to do a profile on a cowboy. Sort of a day in the life of a rancher." Her vague description was meant to entice, her warm smile designed to coax compliance. "Our readers do so admire independent western men."

"Gotta be independent to survive out here, that's for sure." He folded his arms over the front of his black-and-red striped western-cut shirt. "This ladies' magazine you and Katie work on, don't I recollect it's published pretty much all over?"

"In every state. And we've recently gone international. We're currently in five countries. With plans to expand into the former Soviet Union next year."

"Imagine that." He ran a finger over his mustache. "Russkies reading about life on the range."

"I believe it could be our most popular issue." Since she was leaving out a great many pertinent facts, Jude was extremely grateful for an opportunity to tell the unvarnished truth. "After all, the myth of the Wild West is popular all over the world."

Buck cut another look toward Lucky, who'd been rudely rolling his eyes during most of Jude's sketchy explanation. "So, the little lady's gonna be writing about you instead of recipes and housekeeping hints, huh?" His question told Jude that Kate hadn't exactly filled her grandfather in about the editorial content of the magazine. Which wasn't all that surprising. She certainly didn't feel moved to correct the elderly man's misconception.

"We're still in the negotiation stage. I haven't agreed to anything yet."

"Why the Sam Hill not?" Buck looked at his grandson as if suspecting he'd been fed locoweed on the plane. "It'd be good publicity for the Double Ought. And should make those bankers sit up and take notice. Damn easterners," he muttered darkly. Then, as if realizing his mistake, he turned back to Jude. "No offense meant, ma'am."

Her smile didn't waver. "None taken, Mr. O'Neill."

Buck turned to Zach. "Damned if you ain't the spittin' image of an old friend of mine who used to be on the board of the Cattleman's Association, back in our younger years. Name of Jed Newman."

"He's my granddaddy." Zach shook Buck's hand. "I'm Zach Newman. I've been working back east for the past few years."

"Not a lot of cows to wrangle in New York City, I'd imagine."

"No." Zach laughed. "I'm a photographer. I'm hoping to work with Jude on the magazine article."

"The one about the Double Ought?"

"I haven't agreed," Lucky reminded everyone in the room.

Buck ignored him. "Reckon your grandpappy will be real happy to have you back home."

"I imagine he will," Zach said. "He's living on the ranch with my sister and her husband and kids. According to Kayla, he still rides every day with the little mutt collie who's gotta be near as old as him in dog years. I thought I might try to drive up there while I'm here."

"Bet he'd like that. Not that he doesn't have a lot of company already, sounds like. I've got one great-grandson—that'd be my granddaughter Katie's baby boy, Dillon—living clear across the danged country. And this one here—" he tilted his head toward Lucky "—doesn't seem real inclined to do his part to fill the house with kids anytime soon."

"I thought it might be a good idea to find myself a wife first," Lucky said neutrally.

While the men were verbally sparring in a way that had her thinking it was not the first time they'd discussed the subject, Jude took the opportunity to glance around the front room, taking in the well-worn bark brown leather sofa and matching chairs, the pine tables that looked to be handmade, the monk's cloth curtains at the windows.

It was a room designed for comfort, for relaxing in after a hard day's work. It was also definitely a man's room. The only touches of femininity were the copper pot filled with daisies sitting on the coffee table and the needlepoint renditions of deer and elk grazing in mountain meadows hanging on the gleaming pine-paneled walls.

"I love your home. It looks so comfortable." Another absolute truth. Jude decided she was on a roll.

"The place has seen a lot of living in the past seventy-five years," Buck agreed with obvious pride. "Things are slower to change out here than what you're used to, I reckon. In fact, I'm still sleeping in the same room I was born in."

"Imagine that." Jude was suitably impressed. "I may have grown up in New York, Mr. O'Neill, which might make you think we wouldn't have all that much in common. But I can appreciate roots. And now that I've seen your home, I can certainly understand why your grandson was in such a hurry to get back here."

Once again Buck looked over toward Lucky who'd been grinding his teeth as Jude had proceeded to do her best to charm his grandfather.

"By the way," Buck informed his grandson, "Katie did manage to say, before hanging up, that there'd been a little misunderstanding about Jack deserting her and Dillon."

Lucky rubbed his jaw. "I suppose that's one way of putting it." Jude was relieved that he didn't mention his sister's not-so-white lie on her behalf.

"So, she and my great-grandson are okay?"

"They seem to be. So far, anyway."

Lucky studiously avoided glancing over at Jude, who experienced a twinge of guilt that she'd used his loyalty to his little sister as leverage. Then again, she hadn't really been lying. Although she had no concrete proof that Kate's job would be in danger if she was fired, Tycoon Mary certainly hadn't shown any signs of being open-minded since taking over the publisher's office. Kate had vocally backed Jude on every issue; that alone would have put her career in jeopardy.

"Glad you made that banker she married see the light," Buck decided, apparently satisfied with Lucky's less than revealing answer.

Jude found it interesting that the older man had obviously trusted Lucky to fix whatever problem Kate might have had. Such automatic confidence had her experiencing a vague tug of envy. After all, she'd struggled her entire life to win her father's approval. Unfortunately, although she'd managed to escape criticism as she'd gotten older and gained more experience, she couldn't recall her father ever congratulating her on a job well done. That he'd never acknowledged her dedication to the empire he'd created was one of the few failures of her life. And one that continued to hurt.

"I'll bet you're hungry after that long flight," Buck said to Zach and Jude, breaking into her unhappy thoughts. "Since I wasn't sure when you all would get up here from Cheyenne, I made up a mess of my five-alarm chili." He winked. "The good thing about chili is the longer it sits, the better it gets."

"Five-alarm chili?" Jude wondered how many rolls of Tums it would take to put out those particular flames.

"Sounds great," Zach said.

"Buck's chili wins the grand prize ribbon for the hottest every year at the state fair," Lucky assured her. His grin suggested her trepidation hadn't gotten by him. Then again, despite his outwardly laconic attitude, she suspected very little did.

"Is that so? How wonderful." She certainly didn't want to insult Buck O'Neill before she could garner his complete support for her project.

"We think so." Lucky took off his hat and sent it flying across the room where it caught on the wooden hook exactly as he'd planned. The fact that he was enjoying himself immensely at her expense wasn't lost on Jude. "My grandmama Josie used to say it was perfect for stripping paint off the side of the barn."

"My Josie was a real teaser," Buck countered. "Just like her smart-mouthed grandson." He shot Lucky a fondly warning look before turning back to Jude. "Mebe you should put me in your magazine, instead."

Beside her Zach made a sound somewhere between a choke and a laugh.

Feeling she was losing control of the situation again, Jude managed a faint smile. "I think an interview with you would add a lot to the article." It was her turn to slant a wicked grin Lucky's way. "You can tell us all about what kind of boy your grandson was."

"A hellion, pure and simple," Buck said. "Near drove his mama and daddy crazy with his cockeyed stunts. Why, I recollect this one time, when he was six, when he drove the old pickup right through the side of his grandma's henhouse. You've never seen so many feathers fly. We were havin' stewed chicken for weeks after that little adventure."

Jude laughed as she was supposed to. "I've never

had an award-winning dinner before, Mr. O'Neill. It certainly smells wonderful."

"It'll clear your sinuses, that's for sure," Buck said with gusto. "I'll let Lucky show you two upstairs to your rooms so you can freshen up while I spoon it out. Oh, and call me Buck. We're not real formal in this neck of the woods."

This time her smile was sincere. "Thank you, Buck. I'm looking forward to your dinner."

Okay, so it was another lie. As she watched his eyes light up with satisfaction, she assured herself that it was also a harmless one.

Zach nodded to Buck and also turned to leave. There was a little jostling at the foot of the stairs as Lucky, playing the gentleman, stepped back so Jude could precede him and Zach. She, not wanting to give Lucky such an up close and personal view of her bottom, insisted he go first. Unfortunately, he proved more stubborn, and although she was grateful for him not saying a word, she imagined she could feel those brown eyes watching every movement of her hips.

He opened the first door at the top of the stairs. "It's not fancy," he told Zach. "But the bed's firm and the sheets are clean."

"It'll be great." Zach entered the room and tossed his camera onto the bed. "Thanks."

"Yours is right across the hall," Lucky said. "I figured you wouldn't mind staying in Katie's room."

Jude's first impression was that the bedroom had been frozen in time. It was obviously the room of a teenager. Colorful plush stuffed animals covered the canopied bed, photographs were stuck into the white frame of the mirror and a bubblegum-pink-and-white striped comforter covered the mattress. Frilly lace curtains hung at the wall and skirted an antique dressing table.

"My mama's kind of sentimental," Lucky explained as he viewed the obvious surprise on Jude's face. "She's kept it the same as it was when Katie went back east to college."

"I think that's sweet." She paused in front of a blurred photograph of Lucky wearing an American flag shirt and sitting—just barely—atop an enormous Brahma bull. "I'm also impressed."

"Don't be. A second after that picture was snapped, I landed flat on my ass in the dirt."

"That must have hurt."

"Not as bad as when the stupid bovine stepped on my shoulder."

"You're kidding!"

"Here." He reached out, took hold of her hand and brought it to the shoulder in question. "Amazing what they can do with plastic these days, isn't it?"

She could feel the lumps beneath her fingertips and marveled at how much pain he must have been in. Then, against her will, she couldn't help noticing the warmth emanating from his skin through the cotton twill.

"Your mother must have been frantic."

"Nah. She knows injuries come with the territory. After all, she met my dad at a rodeo." Lucky chuckled in a way that Jude knew would have strummed innumerable sensual chords if they hadn't been here in a room radiating Kate O'Neill's youthful innocence.

"She was the nurse working the medical tent," Lucky continued. "He took a dive off a bull and gave himself one helluva concussion. Later he swore he did it just to get her attention."

"Did he?" If Lucky's father had even half the natural charisma Lucky possessed, Jude figured he definitely wouldn't have needed to go flying off any bucking bull to get a woman's attention.

"Mom's always liked to claim that she thought he was too brash, too arrogant and too damn chauvinistic." Lucky's grin touched his eyes, turning them to that lustrous amber gold again. "But they've been together ever since that first day. In fact, in thirty-five years, they've never missed a night sleeping under the same roof."

"That's amazing."

"If you could see them together, you wouldn't find it so amazing. There was a time, back when I was in high school, that it was downright embarrassing to have parents who were so crazy about each other."

His smile turned reminiscent. "There was this one time, during my junior year, when they were roped into chaperoning the homecoming dance. You have no idea how it feels to have all the other kids see your parents slow dancing cheek to cheek."

"No," Jude said softly. "I don't."

The little girl, who'd grown up wishing for two parents who'd love each other and adore her, experienced another little tug of envy. The grown woman struggling to save her career was wondering how she could talk all three O'Neill men into appearing in the article.

Oh, she'd keep the clothes on the older two, of course. But the charisma, not to mention the legacy of the Double Ought that each father had passed on to his son, could make a powerful story.

"Well," he said when a little silence settled over the room, "I'll leave you to your freshening up. This is one of the two bedrooms in the place with its own bathroom. Mom and Dad had it added on when Katie turned thirteen because no one could get into the main one. It's right through there." He tilted his head in the direction of a snow-white door bearing a red-and-white Laramie County High School Mustangs banner, then left the room.

Alone for the first time since she'd gotten up hours earlier, Jude allowed herself a moment to succumb to her exhaustion. She sank down onto the pink-and-white mattress, absently picked up a worn, obviously well-loved stuffed Saint Bernard, and hugged it to her chest as she studied the photo of Lucky hanging on to that huge, bucking bull.

She'd never, in her entire life, met a man like Lucky O'Neill. And she'd certainly never met one who made her feel as if she belonged in this room—as if she were a confused, easily flustered seventeen-year-old girl. Which was strange, because even at seventeen she'd never rattled. Her father had once commented on her having ice water in her veins. That single statement had been the closest thing to a compliment she'd ever received from the larger-than-life man she'd tried so hard to emulate. To please. To, dammit, impress.

"Oh, Kate," she murmured into the Saint Bernard's silky fur, "you were so right. He *is* absolutely perfect."

He was also too appealing for comfort. He had her thinking things she was better off not thinking. Wanting things she'd forgotten she wanted. Deep down, primal things.

When her stomach growled, triggered by the scent of chili that had drifted upstairs, Jude shook her head in self-disgust, tossed the stuffed dog back onto the bed, stood up and marched with a long purposeful stride into the bathroom.

As she washed up and repaired her makeup, she reminded herself that this trip was about *Hunk of the Month* magazine. She'd never allowed herself to mix work and pleasure and she wasn't about to now. Which meant, she warned herself firmly as she followed the appealing tendrils of simmering meat and chili back down the stairs, that a brief hot affair with her next hunk was out of the question.

7

THE LARGE KITCHEN could have come from a country decorating magazine. The cabinets, countertops and large, functional table and chairs taking up the center of the room were pine and, like the coffee table in the living room, seemingly hand-hewn. Cheery red-and-white curtains hung at the windows, copper pots hung above a center island she suspected had been added long after the house was first built. The evening sunset streaming through the windows was tinged with a pink-and-orange hue that made the room appear even warmer. And more cozy.

The huge pot of chili was simmering on a six-burner stove; a plate of fragrant corn bread squares had been placed in the center of the table.

Just the smell of that corn bread had her stomach growling again. "I think I could eat a horse," Jude announced as she entered the room. She was momentarily disconcerted as all three men seated at the table immediately stood up.

"I've known a horse or two in my time that probably deserved endin' up as someone's dinner," Lucky said as he pulled out one of the heavy chairs for her. "But you're safe. Buck only uses beef or elk in his chili."

"That's comforting to know."

"What would you like to drink, Miz Lancaster?" Buck asked. "We've got beer, coffee, iced tea—"

"The iced tea sounds lovely." She smiled up at him, feeling almost comfortable for the first time since she'd gotten the call about Harper Stone earlier this morning. "And please, if we're going to dispense with formalities, it's Jude."

"Like the patron saint of impossible tasks," Lucky murmured as he sat down beside her.

Jude had a very good idea exactly what impossible task he was referring to. Refusing to react to the barb, she smiled sweetly. "Exactly. He's never let me down."

"Yet," her frustrating hunk goaded.

An unbidden spark of temper flared. Not wanting to get into yet another argument in front of the elderly man she was hoping to make an ally, Jude sipped her iced tea, hoping it would help her keep the cool head she'd always been known for.

"So why is the ranch called the Double Ought?" she asked, directing her question to Buck.

"Because in the early days, more than one rancher around these parts got his start with rustled cattle," Buck explained. "There was many a time when my granddaddy, who homesteaded this land, had to protect his herd from rustlers and Indians with his shotgun." He passed her a plate of butter yellow corn bread. "The Double Ought's a size of shot. The name stuck. And it made for an nice enough brand."

"Isn't that interesting." Although she suspected her imagination was running away with her again, she found it not that big of a stretch to imagine Lucky seated astride his horse in front of a herd of cattle, holding a would-be rustler at gunpoint.

She took a square of corn bread from the plate and broke it in half, releasing a burst of fragrant steam. Buck might have been a champion rodeo rider in his time, but Jude soon discovered that no one could fault his cooking.

"Oh, this is wonderful." She actually sighed her pleasure as she took her first bite. "What did you put in it?"

"Nothing special." The older man shrugged. "Just some chopped up jalapeño. And cheese and bacon."

"It's heavenly. Tildy—the cook who's been in our family since my father was a boy—is from Georgia and I didn't think anyone could top her corn bread. But I believe you've just done that."

A red flush that could have been embarrassment or pleasure, or a combination of both, rose from his collar. "Heck, ma'am, uh, Jude, it's just basic family fare."

"Then your family is extremely fortunate. Believe me, Buck, if this corn bread is any example of your culinary talents, you could probably get work at any restaurant in Manhattan."

"Now why in the Sam Hill would I want to do that?" Buck asked as he placed a white pottery bowl of chili in front of her.

Damn. Jude had known the minute she'd heard the words escape her mouth that they were precisely the wrong thing to say. Her only excuse was hunger and jet lag.

"Good point," she agreed. The five-alarm chili was the color of fire and proved every bit as hot. She took a bite, then immediately reached for her tea to cool off her tongue which she could have sworn had just burst into flames.

"I warned you," Lucky, who was sitting beside her, murmured.

"So you did." Recognizing a challenge when she heard one, Jude took another bite of chili. Then another. Strangely, either the first bite had scorched all the taste buds off her tongue, or she began to get acclimated to the flavor, because in no time at all, while everyone ate in comparative silence, she realized she'd finished off the entire bowl.

"You were hungry," Buck said, eyeing her empty dish.

"Starving. But it was terrific. As good—and as hot—as advertised."

"Gal's got good taste," Buck told Lucky. "Which makes me wonder why she'd want to put you in her magazine."

Lucky chuckled. "I've been wondering the same thing."

Deciding that discretion was the better part of valor, Jude opted against reiterating his obvious hunk attributes. But that didn't stop her from noticing the muscled forearms revealed by his rolled-up shirtsleeves.

"We were in a bit of a deadline problem. The man we were going to feature bailed on us and we had to find a replacement at the last minute. Kate suggested Lucky. So, here I am."

Buck rubbed his chin and gave her another of those silent considering looks that reminded her so much of his grandson. "Seems to me you're leaving a bit out of that story."

As Jude scrambled for an acceptable response, Zach, who'd remained silent all during supper, came to the rescue.

"Is that apple pie I smell?"

"Sure is." Western hospitality won over curiosity. For the moment. But from the way his still-bright eyes had narrowed, Jude realized that it was only a matter of time before she'd have to decide exactly how much she was going to tell Buck O'Neill about *Hunk of the Month* magazine.

It was strange; she'd never been ashamed of what she did for a living. Despite disparaging comments from the so-called establishment editors, she'd always been the first to defend the rights of women to have the same opportunity to view the kind of tasteful, erotic photographs of the opposite sex that men had always enjoyed.

Indeed, compared to some of its competitors in the fast-paced, take-no-prisoners, he-who-dies-with-the-most-subscribers-wins world of magazine publishing, *Hunk of the Month* was even fairly tame. As she felt the need to dodge Buck's questions, Jude wondered who she was trying to protect—Lucky or herself?

After she'd turned down the offer of pie, Lucky surprised her by suggesting they take their business discussion out onto the front porch. Wanting to get matters settled one way or the other before morning, Jude readily agreed.

Night had finally fallen; the wide western sky was a vast sea of indigo set with the first stuttering sparkles of early stars.

"You were right," she murmured as she sank down on the cushion of the old-fashioned swing that brought to mind another, simpler, slower time.

"About the chili?"

"No. Well, that too. It was hot. But good." And strangely, it hadn't created the fire in her stomach she'd feared it might. "But I was talking about your sky."

She'd never seen so many stars. In the city, of course, the bright lights overwhelmed them. But even out at the family summer home on South Hampton, she'd never been treated to a view like this. There seemed to be thousands more flickering to life every second.

"Montana may technically be the Big Sky State," she murmured, "but I can't imagine theirs could possibly be any bigger than this."

"Probably isn't. They just claimed early braggin' rights." The swing swayed slightly as he sat down beside her and put his arm around her shoulder with a smooth, natural gesture that suggested this was not the first time he'd sat on this porch with a woman. "A sky like this kinda helps put life into perspective. Makes you remember there are things a lot bigger in the world than your own petty problems."

A few hours ago she would have taken his words personally, experiencing a knee-jerk defensiveness. But she'd already begun to understand that Lucky O'Neill didn't indulge in the type of verbal power jousting she was accustomed to. If he was going to insult you, he'd come right out and say it. He wouldn't beat around the bush.

"I see what you mean." She watched a falling star streak a trail of silver across the ebony velvet canvas of sky. "Too bad the rest of the world can't discover Cremation Creek." Although it was still technically summer, the temperature had dropped several degrees with the setting of the sun.

"I hope we stay a secret. If all those folks moved out here, then they'd just bring civilization—and its ills— right with them."

"Unfortunately, you're probably right."

Another star streaked across the sky. "Quick. Make a wish," Lucky murmured.

"A wish?" She wished, against all reason, that he'd kiss her out here on the porch swing.

"Wishes made on falling stars are the luckiest. Even better than birthday ones."

"Did you make one?"

"Of course." His eyes met hers, and as his gaze slid over her face, the flicker of male interest made her think they may have shared the same wish.

They sat there for a while, rocking slowly back and forth, getting accustomed to each other's company. The only sounds were the click of crickets, the night breeze ruffling the leaves of the huge cottonwood tree shading the porch, the occasional lonely, strangely sad sound of an owl hidden away in the darkness.

"I called Katie," Lucky volunteered after a time.

"I expected you to." Having been taught to trust no one, she would have done exactly the same thing.

"She dodged the subject of Jack's parents being in financial difficulties. Which means, since the girl's never been able to tell an out-and-out lie, you were telling the truth about her needing her job at your magazine."

"She hasn't shared all that much with me, either," Jude said quietly. "I think her loyalty to Jack makes her feel she'd be betraying a family confidence."

"We're her family."

"So are the Petersons now that she's married Jack. I've always had the impression that his parents lead a high-flying life-style. Even though Jack's father never worked."

"Never?" She heard the blatant disbelief in Lucky's tone. "Not a day in his life?"

"No. He didn't have to. Apparently he'd inherited a rather generous trust fund from his grandmother when he was in his teens. The bank managed the money until he came of age, but there was always enough for college, vacation trips to Europe, that sort of thing."

"But what did he *do?*"

"I told you, he didn't have to do anything."

"Maybe the guy didn't have to work for daily wages," Lucky countered. "But what does he do with his time? How does he fill all the hours in a day?"

"Oh." She decided it wasn't really her place to pass on rumors of the elder Peterson's fondness for martinis and Broadway actresses. "I don't know. I suppose he plays tennis, golf, travels. You know." It was her turn to shrug. "That whole routine."

"None of that's routine around these parts," he noted. "And although I get the impression that you were born with a proverbial silver spoon in your luscious mouth, you still work."

He thought her mouth luscious! The knowledge shouldn't cause such a glow of pleasure. But it did. "I can't imagine not working."

"Me, neither." The hand that had been resting lightly on her shoulder tugged on her hair in a casual, unthreatening way. But she knew that once again they were feeling the same thing when his coffee-dark eyes began to steam. "Imagine a country boy like me and a city gal like you having anything in common."

Her throat went strangely dry. She tried to blame her suddenly desert arid mouth on too much salt in the chili, but knew that wasn't really the cause.

"Imagine," she managed to whisper.

"Makes you kinda wonder what else we might find we share. If we were inclined to look."

"Lucky—" she put a hand against the front of his shirt "—I think this is where I tell you—"

He covered that hand with his larger, darker one.

"Let me guess. You're going to tell me that you don't fool around with men you work with."

She swallowed. "That's right. I mean in my business, I meet a lot of men—"

"I'd imagine so." Lucky liked the feel of her hand on his chest, fantasized about it against his bare skin.

"And not just the models," she said, determined to set the record straight right off the bat. "Despite the fact that we're a woman's magazine, there are a lot of men working at *Hunk of the Month*. And although I'll admit to having been attracted to a few of them over the years—"

"That just shows you're normal," Lucky assured her.

"Exactly." Although he still hadn't let her make her point, Jude was relieved that he at least seemed to understand where she was going with it. "But my father always pointed out that mixing business and pleasure only complicates both."

"And from the sounds of it, you're a lady who already has enough complications in her life."

"Yes." She dragged her hand through her hair. "Which is why I vowed early in my career not to allow personal feelings to interfere with my work."

"I'm impressed." And privately relieved to discover that when he did bed Jude Lancaster—which Lucky had every intention of doing—he wouldn't be joining her personal harem of hunks. "So, does this mean that if I agree to be your Hunk of the Month, I can't carry you off to the nearest hayloft like I've been wanting to do since you hijacked my taxi?"

It shouldn't have been such a difficult question to respond to. But heaven help her, as she looked up into Lucky's fathomless dark eyes glinting in the moonlight and recalled her own errant fantasy of making love to him in a fragrant bed of hay, Jude found she couldn't make herself give him the only possible answer.

"You can't tell me you haven't been wondering." His voice was deep and low.

"Wondering what?"

"What it would be like." The soft breeze feathered a few strands of hair across her cheek. When he brushed them away, the touch of callused fingertips against her skin made her go stone still. "Me kissing you." The tantalizing touch skimmed around her jaw. "You kissing me back."

"Lucky—"

"We started out on a lie, Jude." There was a low gruffness to his voice that reminded her of the mating growl of a wolf she'd recently seen on a *National Geographic* program. "Now, since I understand you were in a bind, I'm willin' to wipe the slate clean on yours and Katie's little subterfuge. But I'm going to have to insist that you tell me the truth about this."

Their thighs were touching, side to side, her hand was still on his chest, allowing her to feel the strong steady beat of his heart. His fingers were cupping her chin and their faces were so close together she had to struggle to focus.

"Yes." It was more croak than a proper answer. Jude, who'd never been at a loss for words in her life, tried again. "Yes." She was pleased when her voice was stronger. Steadier. "Of course I have, but—"

"Thank God." She hadn't even been aware he'd been holding his breath until he let it out. "I was beginning to worry that I was the only one going nuts."

He cupped her face between his palms. "There's one thing you should know before I do what I've been wanting to all evening.... I've decided to help you out—"

"You have?"

"Yeah, and we can get into all the whys and wherefores and what limits I'm going to insist on later. Right now I just want you to understand that you don't have to kiss me to convince me to go along with yours and Katie's cockeyed scheme."

"Yes." The single word was a soft, shaky, unfamiliar sound that could have come from the lips of a stranger. "I do."

He smiled at that. With his lips and his eyes. And then slowly, deliberately lowered his head.

Since the attraction she felt for this man had struck like a bolt of lightning from a Wyoming sky, Jude expected his kiss to drag her swiftly into the storm. But his mouth brushed hers lightly, like the welcome touch of a soft summer zephyr. Once, twice, a third time. Each time lingering a bit longer, encouraging her to open to him as a wild rose opens its petals to the enticement of a benevolent sun. Jude could not have denied him, even if she'd wanted to. Which she didn't.

His thumb brushed a gentle pressure against her chin, inviting her lips to part to allow him further intimacy. An intimacy she readily obliged. She felt his soft sigh of satisfaction.

"Ah, Jude." Never had her name sounded so special. So lovely. Like a promise. Or a prayer.

Her eyes were closed, but she could still see the sparkling stars wheeling behind her lids. When he dampened, first her top lip, then the bottom with the tip of his tongue, she felt a warmth encompass her, as though the heat from those pinpoints of fire had enveloped her.

Amazingly, even now, when she would have rushed, he demonstrated a patience that was almost otherworldly. Even as she longed to feel his hands all over her body, they continued to hold her face as his mouth teased and tormented, making her desperate for more.

"Lucky." Her own hands seemed strangely, unnaturally heavy as they lifted and threaded their way through his hair. "Please."

He was drawing things out of her—needs, wants, unruly emotions—with only his mouth. She felt oddly, uncharacteristically shy, both thrilled by the passion his kisses stirred and self-conscious at the same time. "Kiss me."

"That's what I'm doin', darlin'." His warm, wickedly slow lips skimmed up the side of her face, leaving a trail of heat.

"No." Her hands clutched fistfuls of his silk hair, dragging his mouth back to hers. "I mean *really* kiss me."

He chuckled at that. A rich, low rumble that vibrated through her like a tuning fork. "You're definitely a city girl, New York." She felt his smile against her mouth. "Always in such a hurry." Her hands were now fretting up and down his back, like sparrows beating their wings against a hurricane. With a control that on some distant level Jude admired, even as it frustrated, his hands moved with agonizing slowness over her shoulders, warming her flesh beneath her silk blouse.

"Out here in cowboy country, we like to take things slower." His touch barely skimmed the crests of her breasts. "Do things right."

Lucky O'Neill frustrated her. Fascinated her. As she

began to tremble from the power he seemed to wield over her, he also frightened her.

As if possessing the uncanny ability to read her turmoiled mind, he pulled back slightly. Her body felt absolutely bereft as his hands abandoned it to fall lightly to his sides. "We'd better be getting you to bed."

"Bed?" Confusion swirled even as desire continued to drag at her.

"Alone." He skimmed a finger down her nose as he had earlier in an affectionate gesture that was totally at odds with the passion he'd made her feel with that devastatingly slow kiss. "Tomorrow's a big day. We're bringing the bulls down from the summer meadows. I have to get up early and if you intend to go along—"

"What?" She stared up at him. "You want me to go with you on a roundup?"

His expression turned serious. "I can't take the day off, Jude. Not even for you and Katie. Oh, you'll get your pictures," he assured her, effectively cutting off her planned protest. "But since I have to take care of ranch business before I can take off and play hunk for you, I figured you might like to see some real cowhands in action. So you'll have a feel for the work when you write the copy."

She wasn't about to admit that she hadn't planned on all that much copy. After all, although she'd throw herself into Cremation Creek before admitting it, *Hunk of the Month* subscribers did not really buy the magazine for any in-depth articles.

"But we don't have much time."

He clucked his tongue. "There you go, hurrying again, New York. I was talking with Zach while you were freshening up. He says that so long as he has the pictures by next week you'll be able to get the magazine to bed on time.''

''Well, yes, but—''

''So, the way I see it, you've got two choices. You can stay here and get yourself a healthy, mind-clearing dose of fresh air and Buck's country cooking while you're waiting for me to get my work done. Or, you can go on back to New York and Zach will send the pictures when they're done.''

''Zach's a marvelous photographer and I trust him implicitly. But it's my name on the masthead as managing editor and since there isn't any time in the schedule for retakes, I'll feel better if I watch the shoot myself. So, I'll stay.''

What she did not say was that there'd been more than a few photo shoots over the years she'd not bothered to attend. What she tried not to admit, even to herself, was the reason she was finding it necessary to stay in Wyoming for this one was sitting right beside her.

''I was hoping that might be your decision.'' He laced their fingers together and stood up, bringing her with him. ''Buck serves breakfast at five.''

''Five in the morning?''

''It's a little late. But I figured after the long day you've had, you'd need a few hours extra sleep. It's about an hour ride up to the pastures and—''

''Ride?'' She felt a prick of suspicion. ''Surely you mean drive.''

''We'll drive the first few miles. But then we'll have to switch to horses to get the rest of the way up the mountain.''

''I haven't ridden in years.''

''Don't worry, it'll come back to you. Just like riding a bicycle. And after the itty-bitty English saddle you undoubtedly used back in New York City, a western saddle will feel like you're sittin' in Duck's La-Z-Boy recliner."

Jude wasn't all that surprised that he'd guessed right about her saddle. "There's no way I can ride a horse in this suit. And my clothes won't get here until tomorrow, and even then—"

"That's no problem, either." He skimmed a judicious glance over her. "You're about my mom's size. You can borrow some stuff from her closet."

"I'd feel uncomfortable raiding another woman's closet."

"She wouldn't mind. She's always been a big believer in western hospitality. If Mom were here, she'd make the offer herself. Since she's down in Durango with Dad, that leaves me to make you comfortable."

Well. He'd deftly maneuvered his way around every roadblock she'd tried to construct. "This is another little test, isn't it?" Jude asked suspiciously. "To see if you can get the New York City girl to crumble."

"I told you, darlin', I'm not much for playing games. Except for a little slap and tickle from time to time," he amended, allowing his dark eyes to linger wickedly on the lips he'd so thoroughly tasted. "Do you feel as if you might crumble?"

She folded her arms and met his teasing look straight on. "Not on a bet."

"Good." This time he didn't give her any warning. His head swooped down and he captured her lips in a quick, hot kiss that rocked her all the way to her toes and ended far too soon. "I'll say this for you, New York. You've got gumption."

Gumption. Much later, as she lay alone in Kate's narrow single bed, watching the moon move across the sky outside the open window, and listening to the eerie coyote serenade, Jude told herself that the lightly tossed off compliment should not have pleased her so much. But, dammit, for some reason, it had.

Compared to the other men she'd kissed over the years, Lucky O'Neill was laid-back and outwardly easygoing. But he was far from safe.

Yet another important thing to keep in mind, she thought, as she drifted off into a light, restless sleep filled with sensual dreams that had her tossing and turning and tangling the sheets all night long.

8

ALTHOUGH LUCKY WASN'T about to admit it out loud, he was surprised when Jude actually walked into the kitchen the next morning half an hour before their designated departure time, wearing the clothes he'd retrieved from his mother's closet the night before. The well worn jeans were a bit baggy, he considered, as he skimmed a quick glance over her. And the red flannel shirt she was wearing over the T-shirt hung nearly to her knees. Fortunately, they'd determined last night that she and Marianne O'Neill wore the same size boots.

Jude had gathered her pale hair at the nape of her neck with a small gold clip and had sensibly forgone makeup, which, along with the oversize clothes, made her look younger, and a great deal more approachable. And, he thought with a frown, too delicate for ranch work.

She'd been right, of course. When she'd accused him of inviting her to come along on the bull roundup as a test. It had been a challenge Lucky had suspected she wouldn't be able to pass up. At the time, he'd figured that if he was going to be miserable doing something he didn't want to do, then turnabout was only fair play. Call him perverse, but there'd been a part of him that had been looking forward to this city gal's misery.

But now, as he observed the bruiselike purple

smudges beneath eyes that revealed a lack of sleep, Lucky began to have second thoughts.

"You know, it's going to be a long day," he said.

The smile she mustered up was as cool as her gray eyes, reminding him of frost on a pond. "Trying to warn me off, cowboy?"

Lucky shrugged and took a swallow of the coffee Buck had made. It was as black as crude oil, and strong enough to melt a horseshoe, intended to get the blood stirring for the day's work ahead. Lucky knew he was in big, big trouble when just looking into Jude's exquisite, unadorned face stirred up his juices more than the high-octane caffeine.

"Just letting you know what you're getting into. To tell the truth, I didn't expect to see you down here this early."

"I have no idea why." This smile was even frostier than the first.

Once again Lucky found the contrast between the simmering heat she'd displayed last night and this morning's cool control more than a little intriguing. What would it take, he wondered idly, to make her lose that mask of control? That very question had nagged him most of the night.

"I've always been a morning person," she continued blithely. She crossed the room and took the old-fashioned aluminum pot from the stove. "I've always found it extremely gratifying to be getting work done while the rest of the world is still lying in bed."

Lucky didn't know about the rest of the world, but the thought of this particular woman lying amidst rumpled sheets in a warm bed was a far more perilous thought than he wanted to harbor when he was facing a long day's work. He watched her pour the coffee into a chipped mug, saw her eyes widen ever so slightly at the strength of the thick black devil's brew when she took the first sip, and gave her reluctant points when she didn't so much as flinch.

"There's milk in the fridge. And a box of C&H sugar in the cupboard," he offered. "If it's too strong for you."

"Oh, I've always said coffee can't be too strong." She met the faint challenge in his gaze with a level look of her own. "This is absolutely perfect. Just the way I like it."

Her lie was slick as moss on a wet rock and as transparent as glass. Lucky reminded himself that in her high-powered, deal-making publishing business, Jude Lancaster was undoubtedly accustomed to prevaricating on a daily, perhaps even hourly, basis. It was a good thought to keep in mind; it would prevent him from getting all carried away with how strangely right she looked in the O'Neill family kitchen.

"Buck's outside, loading the stuff for the noon meal into his cook trailer," he said. Although some outfits settled for sandwiches for lunch, his grandfather had always believed that feeding the hands cold meals on a roundup was one of the best ways to ensure a mutiny. "But if you don't mind cooking them yourself, there are eggs in the refrigerator. And he left a skillet of fried potatoes and bacon in the warming oven."

"I've never been much of a breakfast eater."

"Breakfast is the most important meal of the day. And you've got a real long one ahead of you. You should eat something."

"How sweet of you to be concerned." Her tone said otherwise. "But really, I'm fine."

Although the two women didn't look a bit alike,

Lucky suddenly realized why Jude had seemed vaguely familiar when he'd first walked into her office. Damned if she didn't remind him of his grandmother. Although Josephine O'Neill had been tall and slender, bringing to mind the willow trees that lined the bank of Cremation Creek, her strong, unyielding personality could have been carved from pure oak.

Even Buck, who'd obviously adored her, had often complained that his hardheaded bride hadn't known the meaning of the word *bend*. Of course, even during those times when she'd tested his exasperation quotient to the limit, Lucky had always detected a note of pride in his grandfather's voice.

Gumption. Josie O'Neill had had it in spades. Although the jury was still out on Jude, Lucky had to admit that so far she wasn't doing too badly. Although he knew it was downright ornery of him, he decided to notch things up a bit. Just to test her mettle.

"I forgot you grew up with a family cook." The faint sarcasm lacing his drawled tone was a challenge in itself. "Guess you never learned how to scramble eggs. If you need any help—"

"Thank you, but that's not necessary." Her chin—which was, he considered, just a tad too strong for traditional beauty—came up in that cute little way that once again made him want to kiss her silly. "I may not be in Buck's league, but I can certainly manage scrambled eggs. If I wanted any. Which I don't because—"

"I know. You're not a breakfast eater." Lucky was beginning to regret he'd thrown down the damn gauntlet. Even though she was going to be mostly observing, it was still going to be a grueling, dusty day.

The last thing he wanted was to be responsible for her fainting from hunger and falling off her horse. He envisioned the army of New York injury lawyers that would probably descend on the Double Ought if this magazine executive so much as broke a fingernail.

"Buck made biscuits." He lifted the basket that was sitting in the middle of the table where last night's corn bread had been. "Why don't you at least—"

"I said I'm not hungry."

Oddly, since she'd been telling the truth about not being a breakfast eater, the aroma of the golden butter-milk biscuits was enough to make her mouth water. But not wanting to back down, since she could sense this was yet another contest, Jude took another longer drink of coffee, as if to prove to him she could, and held her ground. "But thank you for offering."

"You know, Jude," Zach said as he entered the room, looking unfamiliar, and downright sexy, in Wranglers, boots and a faded denim shirt, "like it or not, Lucky's right. You're going to be sorry if you don't eat something. If for no other reason than to protect your stomach lining from that toxic waste Buck calls coffee."

"I have no idea what you're talking about." She smiled over the rim of her mug as she took yet another sip and envisioned it eating away at her insides. Which was, admittedly, not a pretty thought. But the idea of surrender proved even more unpalatable.

A silence settled over the kitchen as Jude and Lucky just looked at each other, like John Wayne and Lee Marvin in *The Man who Shot Liberty Valance*, each wait-ing the other out to see who'd blink first.

"Hell, be as mulish as you want," Lucky growled, his patience nearing the unraveling point. "But just re-member, you can't use your pocket cell phone to call out for bagels once we hit the trail." He pushed his chair away from the table and carried his plate and mug to the dishwasher. "I've got to go hook up the horse trailer. I'll meet you all outside." That said, he strode from the kitchen without looking back. He didn't exactly slam the door behind him. But he did stop just short of it.

"Well." Zach couldn't quite restrain his grin. "That was an interesting little test of wills." He plucked a biscuit from the basket. "And while I can understand why you felt the need to establish control over this situation, I'm surprised you'd risk losing your potential hunk's cooperation before we got him on film."

"He told me last night he was going to do it."

"You know what they say about verbal contracts being worth the paper they're written on."

"He won't back down." Giving in to temptation, now that Lucky wasn't here to witness her surrender, Jude took a biscuit from the basket Zach was holding out to her, broke it open, and slathered it with butter.

"You're so sure of that?"

The biscuit was as light as a fluffy white cloud and tasted like ambrosia. The yellow creamery butter she'd given up years ago caressed her tongue. It was all Jude could do not to moan her appreciation. "Lucky O'Neill is not the kind of man to welsh on a deal."

Zach refilled his mug and held the carafe out to Jude, who refused with a shake of her head. She wasn't sure there were enough biscuits in the entire state of Wyoming to protect her stomach from Buck's thick sludge-like brew. She wondered how it could be that such an excellent cook could make such horrendous coffee.

"O'Neill may not be a welsher, but you realize, of course, that he's going to try to make life as miserable as possible for you today."

"The thought did cross my mind."

"You don't sound all that worried."

"I have to admit that, in a way, he's entitled. After all, I'll be doing the same to him. Once we get to the photo session." She knew she could be considered perverse, but she was actually anticipating bossing a near-naked Lucky O'Neill around.

"But *he'll* be well paid."

"True. But his cooperation, no matter how reluctant, is going to allow me to keep my job," she reminded him. "Besides, I don't think money matters all that much to him."

"Any rancher interested in getting rich ought to get into another business." There was an intensity to his voice that she'd only ever heard before when he'd been talking about framing a shot. Although they'd been on friendly working terms over the years, she was suddenly curious about his former life.

"Do you miss it? Your family's ranch?"

"Not the work. As far as I'm concerned, a cow is about the dumbest animal God ever put down on this green planet, and the best place for it is between two slices of sesame seed bun."

He rubbed his jaw and looked out the kitchen window to the brightly lit gravel driveway where horses were being loaded into trailers for the trip north. "And I damn well don't miss busting my butt sitting on a horse in the pouring rain, tracking down some damn bovine who's found a new hiding place for this year's calf.

"But there are admittedly times when I miss the lifestyle. And I definitely miss the people. I've always thought the best people in the country come from family farms and ranches."

Seeming a bit embarrassed at stating his feelings out loud, he grinned. A grin that, while possessing considerable masculine charm, did not affect her in the same way Lucky's did. "Present company excluded, of course."

She smiled back. "Of course."

The plan, as Lucky explained it when they'd gathered in the circular gravel driveway, was for everyone to drive out to the first pasture, where the portable corrals had already been set up. The corrals would serve as a holding area, he explained to Jude, keeping the bulls in one place while they were being loaded into the stock trailers for the trip down to the lower pastures.

"Isn't that dangerous?" Jude asked as they drove through the predawn dark in Lucky's pickup. "Can't people or horses get gored?"

"It's not like bullfighting," he said. "Our bulls are fairly tame because we bring them down to the bull pastures and feed them all winter. Now sometimes, admittedly, when we get them together they're going to fight. But hopefully they'll settle their differences once they get in the pasture and away from the cows."

"How many are you running?" Zach asked from the back seat.

"We've got five thousand head, which works out to just short of one hundred and fifty bulls."

"Is that enough? My daddy always said that bulls are like good cowpunchers—if you've got enough of them, they'll make you money."

"Oh, Lord," Jude said on a groan, "not you, too. Is there something in the water out here that makes men feel the need to quote western wisdom?" The idea that this man she'd always considered the epitome of eastern seaboard sophistication even fit the description of a cowboy still continued to amaze her.

"It's called lore," Lucky advised her. "Knowledge out here tends to get passed down from father to son, through the generations. In the olden days, you couldn't go off to college to study ranching. And even now that you can, the most valuable lessons come from experience."

Jude had gotten sidetracked on one part of his answer. "You can actually go to college to learn to be a cowboy?"

"A rancher. There *is* a difference."

She wasn't about to get into an argument over semantics. "Did you? Go to college?"

He shrugged. "Sure."

"What was your major?"

"I've got a bachelor's degree in range management. And a masters in holistic resource management."

Although she was admittedly surprised, his casual answer didn't come as quite the revelation it might have twenty-four hours ago. "I knew it!"

"What?"

"That the dumb cowpoke act was exactly that. An act."

Actually, now that the subject had come up, Lucky considered apologizing for having misled her. He certainly wouldn't like anyone pulling his leg like he'd been doing. But then again, he considered, she kind of deserved it after treating him like some bull she'd been considering buying. The way she'd checked him over, he was surprised she hadn't ordered him to drop his pants right there in that blinding snow field she called an office.

"You were saying about the bulls?" Zach interjected

smoothly, his deft change of subject earning a grin in the rearview mirror from Lucky and a frown over her shoulder from Jude.

"The majority of folks around these parts run an average of one bull per twenty, twenty-five cows. Some, believing like your dad did, even go as high as six bulls per hundred. But I've been keeping the numbers the past few years and once we started using mature, semen-tested bulls, we were able to cut back to one bull to every thirty-five head.

"Of course we have to keep more coming all the time because we tend to cull them younger than some outfits."

"Why is that?" Jude asked.

"Seems that by the time a bull's six to eight years old he just loses interest in his work and spends most of his time hanging around the water. Or lying in the shade. Then he's got to go."

"That's pretty harsh, isn't it?"

"It might sound like it to someone who's grown up not giving a lot of thought to where her dinner comes from," Lucky agreed. "But the fact of the matter is that although no rancher's in the cow business to make a lot of money, he can't afford to lose a lot, either." His words seconded what Zach had told her earlier. "If a bull isn't taking care of business—if he isn't romancing the cows—well, he sure isn't doing the Double Ought much good."

As a businesswoman, Jude reluctantly saw his point. But still... "How fortunate for you that you weren't born a bull."

He flashed her a rakish grin she was quite certain had caused more than one Wyoming woman's toes to curl in her cowboy boots. "Honey, the day I get too old to romance a willing female is the day they'd better start measuring me for a pine coffin. Because there won't be any reason for me to get up in the morning."

"You really are impossible," she muttered, fighting back a smile.

"And you really are as cute as a newborn foal in that getup. Kinda makes me wonder if we've got things a little back-asswards around here."

"What does that mean?"

"Perhaps you should be the one taking your clothes off for the camera. And I should be the one checking for flaws, frostbite and sunburn."

"Impossible," she repeated. As Zach chuckled appreciatively from the back seat, she turned away, pretending a vast interest in the scenery out the passenger window.

In truth, she didn't have to pretend. The mosaic of towering gray granite mountains, lush green fields and deep blue lakes fed by glaciers high in the mountains was stunning. And vastly quiet. There were no sounds of traffic, no sirens, no horns blaring, no banging of trash cans in the early morning stillness. It was strange, almost otherworldly. And wonderfully peaceful. She could almost feel her heartbeat slowing.

"I'm beginning to understand why *Close Encounters* was set here."

He gave her a sideways glance. "Stands to reason it'd be easier to set a spaceship down with all this wide-open space than try to land in Times Square."

"Of course," Zach drawled, "if an alien wanted to go undetected, he'd probably be better off heading for Manhattan. Who'd notice a few more weird life-forms in Times Square?"

Jude laughed at that, as she was meant to. But as she

compared the two so dissimilar places she wondered if Kate ever felt claustrophobic in her adopted home.

"Yeah, we wondered about that, too," Lucky agreed when she mentioned it. He rubbed the square jaw Jude noticed he hadn't bothered shaving this morning. "Especially since she always seemed to like ranch life. She was, back in high school, one heck of a barrel racer. I finally decided that my baby sister choosing to go live in that urban anthill you all call home definitely proves the power of love."

Jude thought of the way Kate's face lit up whenever Jack's name was spoken, about the way her expression turned absolutely beatific whenever she mentioned Dillon, which she did, constantly.

"I think you may be right," she said consideringly.

"I know I am. And that's the only reason I didn't do what Buck advised in the beginning and lasso the girl and drag her back home the day she decided to move in with Peterson."

"Kate's not exactly a girl," Jude felt obliged to remark. "She's a wife and mother. And a career woman."

"That may be. But she'll always be my baby sister."

Which was, of course, Jude thought, the reason she was sitting here in the pearlescent yellow glow of early morning light, in a pickup racing down the nearly deserted highway that wound through the pine-covered mountains like a shiny black ribbon. Because this hunky cowboy definitely had a soft spot in his heart when it came to his family.

Having watched an often exhausted Kate struggling to juggle a rising career, a home, new husband, pregnancy and now a child, Jude had always considered herself fortunate that she had no one to be concerned about but herself, no life to worry about but her own. She'd never—not once—envied her assistant. Until now.

Although it might technically be the middle of summer, Lucky had kept heat blasting out of the dashboard vents. When she stepped out of the truck and was hit with a gust of icy air, Jude sucked in a breath.

"It feels like winter." Although she'd thought it was overkill, she was definitely grateful for the flannel shirt and fleece vest Lucky had insisted she put on.

"If it was winter, we'd have never made it up here," he said. "The meadows would be waist-deep in snow. But you should be grateful. If it was as warm up here as it is down in the valley, you'd spend the day battin' mosquitoes."

He reached into the back of the truck, took out a black felt hat and plunked it down on her head. "Here. This'll help keep your body heat from escaping."

"So would getting back in the truck and keeping the heater running all day," she muttered.

"If you don't think you're up to this, I can have Buck drive you back to the ranch," he offered as he pulled on a pair of brown leather gloves.

He had, of course, just hit her most vulnerable spot. Her ego. She tossed her head. "Not on your life, cowboy."

He grinned as if he'd expected just that answer. "Anyone ever tell you that you're awfully bullheaded, New York?"

"Not in those words. But I think you may have just hit on one more thing we have in common."

He rubbed his chin again as he considered that. "Guess it just might be. If we were keeping score."

"Which we're not," Jude said quickly. Too quickly,

she realized when he flashed one of those annoying, knowingly masculine grins.

"Why don't you speak for yourself, darlin'?" he drawled pleasantly. He tugged on the end of a pale blond strand of hair that had escaped the clip at the nape of her neck, adjusted her hat more to his liking, then, seemingly satisfied, walked away with a smooth gait.

It was going to be worth it, Jude reminded herself firmly. She could put up with this man's chauvinism, his teasing, his cocky masculine self-confidence. She could even put up with the cold and the prospect of spending the day sitting on a horse. Because in the end, she was going to go back to Manhattan with a cover article and centerfold that would set the standard for hunkdom into the next millennium.

And then, she thought with a satisfied inner smile, the publishing world would be her own private oyster. She could take those circulation numbers anywhere in the business, parlay it into a VP spot somewhere. Maybe even work up to publisher.

And then, finally, perhaps her father would be proud. That fleeting hope was instantly dashed as she remembered he wouldn't be around to witness her victory. When she felt the sting of tears begin to burn behind her lids, Jude wondered when she'd stop feeling like an orphan.

"There it is again."

The deep voice dragged her from her unhappy thoughts. "There *what* is?" she snapped.

"That little line you get right between your eyes when you frown." Lucky skimmed a fingertip down the crease in question. "And two little ones right here." He touched first one side of her mouth, then the other.

"Didn't your mama ever tell you that's a good way to get wrinkles?"

She batted at the gloved hand that was still on her face. "Since my mother died before my sixth birthday, I don't recall much of anything she might have said."

He took his hand away without argument. "I didn't know, Jude. I'm sorry."

"So was I."

His expression seemed to sober as he gave her another one of those long, judicial perusals. A strange, new kind of silence stretched between them. Then, just when Jude was certain Lucky was on the verge of saying something important, he simply put a friendly arm around her shoulder.

"Let me introduce you to Lightning," he said.

"Lightning?"

"The mare I picked out for you. I think you're going to like her."

She looked at the narrow dirt trail that seemed to climb straight up the side of the mountain. "That name doesn't exactly give me a great deal of confidence. Especially since I have to admit, this looks a bit more difficult than riding in Central Park."

"That's why I picked her for you. She really is a sweetheart. And as gentle as an old dog, despite her name, which we only gave her because her white blaze looks kinda like a lightning bolt. Believe me, New York, when you're sitting in that nice wide western saddle with the tall roping horn to hang on to, you'll feel as safe as if you're riding in your daddy's minivan."

"My father never owned a minivan."

The strange, unsettling mood vanished, like patches of alpine snow melted by a bright hot sun. His grin returned. "Now why doesn't that surprise me?"

9

BY THE END of her first full day on the Double Ought, Jude was definitely wishing that horses came with instrument panels, so she could monitor the odometer to see how far she'd ridden. She'd never realized exactly how wide and open the western rangeland was until Lucky O'Neill had apparently decided to drag her all over every damn inch of it.

Determined to pass whatever macho tests he'd apparently decided were necessary to pay her back for the way she'd disrupted his life, she managed, somehow, to stick by him like the strips of bright yellow flypaper she'd seen in the barn.

She had to admit that the Wyoming high country scenery was spectacular. But as she dragged her aching body out of Kate's cotton-candy-striped pink sheets on the second day of the roundup, the suspicious New Yorker in her continued to suspect that the man was trying to run her off by making life as miserable as possible.

After a quick shower, she dressed in Lucky's mother's working clothes; although Kate had sent her clothes as instructed, the casual outfits that had been so right for the city were obviously unsuitable for such difficult physical work.

Not wanting Lucky to gain the upper hand by leaving without her, she rushed downstairs to the kitchen and chugged down some of the black sludge Buck called coffee, even as she considered it'd probably be more efficient just to inject the caffeine straight into her veins. After forcing down the breakfast she'd discovered yesterday that she did, indeed, need, she climbed into the truck for the ride back up to the pastures. It would be another long grueling day watching a bunch of men in cowboy hats round up some bulls who were equally determined to range free.

On the first day, Jude had been a white knuckle rider.

"You know," Lucky had drawled as he'd observed her literally hanging on to the high western saddle horn, "you don't have to choke that poor horn to death. Why don't you loosen up and let it breathe a mite?"

That was easy for him to say, she'd thought as the docile mare had picked her way around granite boulders, deftly climbing up the steep mountainside. But this morning, her nervousness eased enough to allow her to enjoy the spectacular sight of the colorful mix of riders and what Zach told her were Angus, black baldie and red Herefords spread out over the meadows and canyons. The scene was made complete with the mountains and expansive blue sky as a backdrop.

Jude quickly discovered that despite what Zach had told her about a cow's lack of intelligence, every so often a bull would figure out why all these men on horseback had gathered in his pasture and would take off for the north forty before the crew could get him into the trailer.

Such behavior was always met by cursing and other outward signs of masculine frustration, but Jude couldn't help noticing that the tougher things got, the calmer Lucky became.

"The trick is to move slowly," he explained over a lunch of melt-in-the-mouth tender barbecue beef sandwiches after spending nearly two hours getting some particularly reluctant bull into the pen. "If you chase him too hard, he'll take off, and given enough time, cattle will outrun you, and pretty soon you're out there making an ass of yourself and killing your horse. Each of these guys weighs about a ton, which means he can go damn near anywhere he wants. The trick is to get him to want to go where we want him to."

As the hours passed, Jude and Lightning began to relate to each other, allowing her to gain more and more confidence. Enough so that she enjoyed the afternoon lope across the lush green pasture so much that when it came time to quit for the day, she didn't really want to get off the horse.

It was dark by the time they reached the ranch. The adrenaline of the day had begun to wear off, and she felt a renewed ache in muscles she hadn't even known she had two days ago. It was all Jude could do to keep her eyes open as she ate two bowls of the leftover chili Buck heated up.

Lucky stopped her after supper. "I thought you could use this." He was holding out a brown bottle.

"What is it?"

"Liniment. It'll help get the kinks out."

"What kinks?"

From the back and forth movement of his jaw, she suspected Lucky was grinding his teeth. "The ones from spending the day in the saddle when you're not used to it. But if you're going to start acting like some damn mule again—"

"No." She grabbed the bottle, willing to accept whatever scant comfort he was offering. "Thank you. I am a little stiff."

"That's not surprising. Want some help rubbing it on?"

The fact that his seductive grin failed to stir a single feminine chord proved exactly how exhausted she was. "No, thank you. I can manage."

That stated, she forced her saddle-sore body upstairs. She managed to brush her teeth, strip off her clothes and rub on the oil that made her smell like something that belonged stabled in the barn, before falling into the narrow bed.

The only good thing about such a deep, almost drugged sleep, she considered when her alarm shattered the quiet dark the following morning, was that her exhaustion had kept her from dreaming of Lucky.

Unfortunately, her rebellious mind refused to surrender thoughts of him during the third day of the roundup. As she sat astride the placid, ill-named Lightning, watching Lucky go one on one with a pair of recalcitrant bulls, Jude found herself daydreaming of him in the most outrageous scenarios.

She pictured him stripping off her clothes in the flowered meadows, imagined sitting face-to-face on his lap, making love with him as his mare galloped through the forest. Never mind that such a scenario was probably physically impossible; after all, a more prudent woman would consider this entire outdoor western adventure to be impossible.

He'd definitely not been exaggerating when he'd warned her that the Double Ought wasn't a dude ranch. But, refusing to run up the red flag of surrender, she clung stubbornly to her determination even as she occasionally longed to be pampered.

Late in the afternoon, she caught a glimmer of something on the horizon that looked vaguely familiar. Moments later, she caught a whiff of smoke and realized she wasn't alone when Lightning's eyes widened and rolled back.

Jude rode over to where Lucky and Zach were just finishing herding another bull into the pen. "Is that what I think it is?"

Lucky followed her gaze to where the high green meadow light refracted the haze of faraway forest fires. "A lightning bolt must have struck a tree," he murmured. "Or, sometimes we'll get a fire from a cinder spark from a passing train, but not usually this high up."

"A fire?" A deep-seated fear sent a chill skimming up her spine, through her veins, causing an involuntary tremor.

"It's wildfire season," he told her with a casualness that she couldn't share. "We've been lucky the past two years and haven't had more than a few hundred acres burned. Which, in the long run, actually helps the grasslands."

Fire. It was the one thing—the only thing—that Jude was terrified of. Even now she could remember that horrific night, the sirens, the acrid smoke burning her lungs, her father carrying her out of the house, then rushing back in for her mother....

"People who only see forest fires on the evening news get skewed ideas of them," Lucky was saying, oblivious to the fears curling through her.

Jude tried to close the door on those painful memories, struggled to listen to his explanation, hoping to find some scant assurance that she need not worry. That the distant fire would never come their way.

"Grass has shallow roots and in this part of the country, we just don't get enough steady rain or snow to percolate the ground, so what little moisture we get just passes through the soil, leaching the nutrients too deep for the roots to reach.

"But the trees have longer taproots, so they soak up all the nutrients. Two hundred years ago, the Indians knew enough to oxidize this land. Every twenty years or so, they'd burn the fields, which was why, when the white man first showed up, he was amazed at all the rolling hills of grass as high as a horse's knees. Modern so-called conservation methods of putting out too many fires are the reason we have all these trees and brush."

He pointed to a spot on the high meadow where the grass seemed a deeper, more emerald green. "See that?"

"It looks as if you've fertilized it," Jude said, her interest in the topic helping to sidetrack her fear.

"Mother Nature did. When she burned it last year."

"Did you have to reseed?"

"Nah. The land reseeds itself. That's one of the tricks Mother Nature has up her sleeves. And the fires can't destroy whatever seeds are already in the soil."

She could see his point. Still, Jude thought, as she glanced nervously in the direction of the distant haze, she'd just as soon no "oxidizing" took place while she was on the Double Ought.

Try as she might, Jude couldn't dismiss the ever-present threat of wildfire. It billowed in her mind like smoke while she rode the range with the men. And even though she enjoyed the magnificent scenery, a deep-seated fear disrupted her normally laserlike concentration as she tried to learn more about the actual day-to-day operation of the Double Ought.

"There's something I don't understand," she said on the evening of her fifth day in Wyoming, her fourth spent up in the pastures. She'd tracked Lucky down in the barn where the aroma of horse and hay and the tang of testosterone-laced male sweat hovered in the air like heat lightning. Lightning she was doing her best to ignore.

"Ask away."

She watched him pouring the grain into the horse troughs, noticed the way he had a small word, a gentle touch, a rub behind the ear for each cow pony in turn. That the animals loved him was more than obvious by their eager whinnies, the way they'd curl their lips back in almost a smile whenever he'd approach their stalls. That Lucky loved them back was equally apparent.

"I was reading something in Buck's *Western Horseman* magazine—it was just lying on the table," she said, defensively as he shot her an amused look. "Anyway, there was an article stating that more and more modern ranchers are using helicopters to sight out the livestock. And pickups and four-wheel drive bikes to gather them up. But you're still using horses."

"A lot of guys have gone to that kind of operation," he agreed. "But personally, I don't subscribe to it because like so many other supposedly quick fixes, it's not perfect. You miss too much while you're sitting in a pickup, like a sick calf in the brush, or a cow hiding in a canyon.

"We also use draft horses hitched up to sleds to feed the cattle during the winter, which cuts down on labor costs because one man can feed the stock, whereas if you use a tractor or truck you need an extra man to drive it. There's also the fact that using horses is good for the environment because it cuts down on fossil fuel."

"Plus the fact that you like horses," she suggested.

"Called that one right. Actually, I flat-out love the animals. Buck's always said that there's nothing better for the inside of a man than the outside of a horse."

His gaze shifted out the barn door to the fields of hay illuminated by the full moon overhead. "And on a purely aesthetic basis, it's impossible not to enjoy the scent of the grass or the sight of a red-tailed hawk or bald eagle circling in the sky overhead. Part of the trouble with the modern world is that people are hurrying too fast through life. They don't take time to enjoy the scenery along the way."

For not the first time since she'd arrived in Wyoming, Jude compared Lucky's life with her own hectic life-style in New York and decided that they couldn't be more different. It was, she reminded herself, a fact she'd be wise to keep in mind.

"But not every place has such spectacular scenery to appreciate," she remarked.

"That's true enough, I suppose," he said with a faintly sheepish grin as he turned toward her. "I've always thought that red cattle grazing on green grass is one of the prettiest sights in the world. There's just something about watching them munching the grass, flicking their tails at flies, the calves butting heads, that makes you feel as if everything's right with the world.

"And speaking of pretty sights..." He tipped his hat back and studied her with unmistakable interest. "I've been thinking a lot about that kiss we shared."

"Really?" It took an effort to keep her tone cool

while desire was curling like a lazy cat inside her. "I never would have suspected that. Since you've hardly said two personal words to me during the entire roundup." The complaint, which she'd never meant to reveal out loud, was edged with feminine pique.

"I've been a little busy," he drawled unnecessarily. "And I seem to remember you saying something about not mixing work and play."

"I did."

His lips quirked. "Now why do I hear a *but* in that?" He put down the feed bag. "But now that we've got the bulls in, perhaps I can begin making up for lost time." Her boots felt nailed to the floor as he took two steps to close the distance between them. "You want some pretty words?"

"No." She didn't utter a word of protest as he ran his hands over her shoulders, down her arms, then linked their fingers together. "Because even if we were to get involved, which we both know we shouldn't, I'm a big girl, Lucky. I wouldn't need them."

"That's what you say. But I've never met a woman who didn't like being romanced."

"I was brought up to be a realist." And she was determined to remain one even if there was something about this wide-open land—and the one-of-a-kind man who obviously loved it so—that encouraged foolish romantic fantasies. "I understand that what we're feeling has nothing to do with romance. It's lust, pure and simple."

"It may be lust." He lifted their joined hands and brushed a light kiss against her knuckles. "But believe me, darlin', there's absolutely nothing simple about it."

He wondered what she'd say if he admitted to the

thoughts he'd had as he'd watched her ride over the meadows today: how strangely right she'd looked on his land. But just because she sat well on one of his horses didn't mean she'd fit into his life, Lucky reminded himself. He'd never met a woman who was more city; he was country. He'd be wise to keep that in mind.

"You're right, of course." She reclaimed her hand with a sigh. "You'll have to excuse me. I haven't really been myself lately. The past few months have been a very stressful time for me and I think I may be having a nervous breakdown."

"Sorry, New York." He rubbed at the faint furrows that were etching their way between her brows again. "But we don't allow people to have nervous breakdowns in Wyoming. It ruins our laconic cowboy image."

Jude felt herself strangely torn between the need to laugh and the urge to cry. She was confused, exhausted and, she thought, stressed out to the max. This was absolutely no time to add the complication of an affair into the mix. Not that going to bed with Lucky would lead to a full-fledged affair, she reminded herself firmly. It would be more like an extended one-night stand, lasting only as long as her time in Wyoming.

For some unfathomable reason, it was this thought that caused her eyes to fill with the hot moisture that had been stinging behind her lids. An errant tear escaped to trail down her cheek. With a tenderness she'd never experienced from anyone, Lucky brushed it away with his knuckle.

"It's late. And you've had a physically demanding few days. You'd better get into bed."

She nodded. And, feeling ridiculously fragile, sniffled. "I feel so foolish. You undoubtedly think I'm a weak, overly emotional female."

"No. I think you're an extremely desirable female. I also think you've been too tightly wound for too long and it's inevitable that you'd eventually start to unravel."

His fingers trailed around her jaw and cupped her chin, holding her embarrassed gaze to his sympathetic one when she would have looked away. "Why don't you sleep in tomorrow?"

"I can't. Now that you've finally gotten the bulls in, we need to get started shooting—"

"There's still time. I promise, Jude, you'll get your shots. But a few hours one way or the other aren't going to make any difference in the entire scheme of things."

"It must be nice to be able to be so cavalier about work and deadlines and live so apart from the petty problems the rest of the world has to deal with," she snapped.

Personally, Lucky decided that if Jude thought her work at *Hunk of the Month* magazine had anything to do with the problems of the world, she was in a sorrier mess than he'd suspected. But he decided that this wasn't the time to get into an argument over the subject.

"Cowboys don't spend a whole lot of time sitting around worrying about the meaning of life," he countered easily. "Or talking about it. We live it."

Then, because it had been too many days since he'd kissed her, and because he'd awakened each morning as hard as a damn ramrod because of his hot dreams about her, Lucky ducked his head and covered her mouth with his.

Unlike his first kiss, when he'd coaxed her slowly, inexorably into the mists, this time Jude found herself instantly dragged into the flames. His mouth was hard, demanding, and hers yielded.

Lucky ached as he'd never ached before. And not just the physical ache that had him as hard as a boulder, but a deep grinding need that went all the way to the bone. He wanted her as he'd never wanted another woman. Lord help him, he needed her as he'd never needed any other woman.

The fact that she was totally wrong for him—in every way—did not matter to his throbbing body, reeling mind, or tumbling heart. The fact that there would not be—could not be—anything permanent between them meant nothing. As he tasted a passion sweeter than honey, the future held no meaning, all his yesterdays spun away and there was only now. Only this frozen perfect moment with this incredible female who matched him as no other ever had.

Jude didn't know how it had happened. One minute they'd been discussing ranching techniques, the next minute she was being swept away by a force as wild as the surrounding land. Struggling to keep her equilibrium, she grasped hold of his upper arms and felt muscles like granite clench beneath her fingertips. His thumb tugged, not forcefully, on her chin, coaxing her mouth open to the invasion of his tongue. She tasted coffee. And the cinnamon gum he chewed in place of the tobacco so many of the other cowboys favored. She also tasted a male hunger that had her moaning in response.

When he wrapped an arm around her, pulling her

closer, holding her against him, hard chest to soft curves, she went, willingly. Eagerly. Her hands fretted up and down his back, then knocked off his hat in their desperate need to tangle in his hair.

Even as needy as she was, Jude couldn't help stiffening at the feel of his hands on the front of the western-style shirt.

"It's okay," he crooned, in that same coaxing voice she'd heard him use to talk his mare into crossing a rushing icy stream. "I just want to touch you, Jude." His lips skimmed up her face, nuzzled that unbearably sensitive spot behind her ear. "I've been going crazy, imagining the feel of your body."

"You haven't been the only one." She voiced her compliance on a soft, ragged moan. "I've been imagining the same thing."

When she heard him exhale a deep breath of relief, she realized, on some distant level, that he was not as self-confident, as cocky, as she'd believed.

The overhead lights in the barn were blindingly bright compared with the star-spangled darkness just outside. He didn't take his eyes from hers as he unfastened each white plastic button with a deft touch that made her wonder how many women he'd undressed in this very same barn. Jude found herself longing for the flickering glow of candlelight, or perhaps the flattering light of a crackling fireplace.

"I knew it," he murmured as he folded back the teal-black-and-white patterned material.

"Knew what?" she managed to gasp. As his hands cupped her breasts, causing the nipples to strain against the lace, she could barely breathe. Hardly think.

"That you'd be absolutely perfect." He lowered his head, warming her aching breasts with his breath.

Then, when he opened the front clasp of her bra, his tongue dampened flesh that was so burning hot Jude was amazed she couldn't hear it sizzle.

Wanting, needing to touch him, as he was touching her, to taste as he was tasting, she ripped at his shirt, blessing whoever had put snaps on cowboy shirts. She splayed her hands against his chest, felt the heat emanating from his hard male body and hungered as she'd never hungered for anything or anyone in her life.

As his mouth scorched her breasts and his hands, delving between denim and skin to cup her in an intimate way that made her feel as if she were burning from the inside out, Jude knew that need this intense could not continue to be reined in. Pleasure this rich could not be contained.

For days he'd been chipping away at her restraint, like the jagged mountains ringing the ranch had been chiseled away by eons of harsh environmental forces. Although she'd been unnerved by the way her rigid, hard-fought-for self-discipline seemed to have been eroding ever since Lucky O'Neill had sauntered into her office, she was terrified by this devastating lack of control.

If he took her control, he'd take everything she'd worked to become. And then, Jude thought, there'd be nothing left. Nothing but an empty shell.

Lucky's whole being was focused solely on pleasuring this woman. She was so hot. So ready. As the wet warmth flowed like liquid sunshine over his caressing fingers, Lucky felt Jude tremble. At first he thought it was from desire, but then, as he felt the soft flesh beneath his mouth chill, he realized that somewhere, somehow, along the way, passion had metamorphosed to anxiety.

"I'm sorry." He removed his hand from her jeans, refastened her bra, tucking her breasts away with a look of regret, and began buttoning her shirt with fingers that were far more steady than hers. "I didn't have any right to do that."

"That's funny." Her laugh was weak and shaky. "It sure felt as if you did." The admission caused a flare of hot flames in his eyes, a reaction that drew a groan from her. "I'm sorry. I can't believe I keep giving you these mixed messages. Kiss me. Don't kiss me. Touch me. Don't. It's only business. It's lust." She dragged her hands through her tousled hair. "I'm not only going crazy, I've regressed to sixteen years old."

He surprised her by laughing at that.

"Would it make you feel any better if you knew that I had more control over my body—and my mind— when I was a randy boy of seventeen than I do whenever you get anywhere within kissin' distance?"

"I don't know." She forced herself to meet his friendly gaze when, coward that she'd become, she would have preferred to look away. "I've never been one to take sex casually."

"Yet another thing we have in common," Lucky said. "If we were counting. Which we're not," he said before she could. The hell they weren't, he thought.

"No. We're not." Great. Jude groaned inwardly. After three days of relative honesty, she'd reverted back to lying. So much for progress.

"This can't go anywhere," she said firmly, making Lucky wonder which of them she was trying to convince. "Our lives are light-years apart."

"In every way," he agreed helpfully.

"It's foolish—and dangerous—to have an affair with someone you work with."

"Especially if you're working with other cowboys, horses and cattle."

She laughed. "I finally understand why Kate loves her big brother so." The instant she heard the *L*-word escape her lips, she longed to pull it back. "I mean, I can see how anyone would like you, admire you—"

"You don't have to explain." Her hands, which he'd noticed were seldom still, had begun fluttering in the air between them like sparrows caught in a hurricane. He gathered them into both of his. "I know what you mean." He lifted her hand to his mouth as he had earlier, the light touch of his lips feeling like sparks against her skin.

"I have a suggestion," he offered.

As she looked up into his warm brown eyes, Jude once again felt as if she were ceding control. And once again, the thought terrified her.

"You've got a point about mixing work and fun. So, the next couple of days, while Zach takes my picture for your magazine, why don't you and I spend our spare time just getting to know one another? Trading life stories. Comparing favorite books, movies, that sort of thing. The way a man and a woman who are attracted to each other might do if they were going out on a normal date."

"That sounds like a sensible suggestion."

"I kinda figured you'd think so." He bent down, retrieved his hat from the floor between them, dusted the straw dust off and put it back on his head. Then he gave her a slow, sexy wink. "And then, once we've dispensed with the formalities, and finished up with the work, we can get naked and roll around in the hay."

She felt the uncharacteristic color flood into her face yet again. And it was ridiculous the way he could fluster her with little more than a seductive suggestion or sexual innuendo. Deciding it was time to garner some scant control over the situation, she lifted her chin and returned his teasing gaze with a calm look of her own.

"I'll think on that," she said, using his words.

His grin was quick, pleased and warm enough to make her feel in danger of melting into a little puddle of need. "Why don't you do that?"

He ducked his head and gave her another quick kiss that was as gentle as the fluttering touch of butterfly wings, as warm as buttery July sunshine, and managed to start up the trembling all over again.

"Sweet dreams, New York. I'll see you in the morning. And sleep in. Because believe me, you'll be needing your energy."

There'd been a time, only days ago, when Jude would have taken Lucky's words for a threat. But as she slid between the newly laundered sheets that smelled of fresh mountain air and sunshine, she decided to take them as a promise.

10

Jude couldn't believe it when she looked at the clock the following morning and realized she'd slept a full ten hours. Embarrassed at being thought of as lazy, she showered and dressed quickly. Buck was alone in the kitchen, cutting up stew meat, when she entered.

"Good morning," she greeted him.

"Morning." His bright eyes narrowed as they skimmed over her face. He nodded his approval. "You're looking a lot more chipper this morning."

She was grateful to him for not pointing out that it was nearly afternoon. "I can't remember the last time I slept this late."

He shrugged in a way that reminded her of Lucky. "I'll bet you can't recall the last time you pushed your body as hard as you have the past few days, either." He poured coffee into a mug and put it in front of her. "Cowboying is hard work. It takes some getting used to."

"I'm finding that out."

"But you've been a real trooper. A lot of women would have quit the first day."

"I'm not a quitter."

"Seems not," he agreed. "Your folks must be mighty proud of you."

"My parents aren't living."

"Now that's a real shame." He rubbed his jaw and

studied her for a longer time. "You got family back east? Brothers, sisters, aunts or uncles?"

"No. I was an only child. And what relatives I do have I never see. We weren't exactly a close family."

And that had never bothered her. Until now. She took a sip of Buck's black battery acid and wondered if he'd made it a bit weaker this morning. Or perhaps she was actually getting used to it.

"Coffee too strong for you?" he asked, as if reading her mind.

"Not at all."

"Got the recipe from my daddy. It's kind of a modern version of the old cowboy roundup coffee where you'd take a pound of coffee, wet it good with water, then boil it over a hot fire. After a time you pitched a horseshoe in. And if it sank, you dumped in more coffee."

"And if it melts, it's just right," she guessed.

He laughed appreciatively. "You've got gumption, all right, gal. You'll be wanting some breakfast."

"Although it seems decadent to be having breakfast at this hour, I believe I would, thank you." She'd have to stop eating like this once she returned to her sedentary New York life or she'd weigh more than King Kong. "You really are a wonderful cook," she offered as she watched him pour the pancake batter onto the sizzling skillet.

"My daddy always told me that well-fed crews work better, and I can't say he's been proven wrong. In the old days, most ranchers made sure that every hand workin' a spread had a bedroll, slicker, guns and ammunition, plenty of tobacco and, of course, hearty food."

"That's probably not a bad benefit package," she

said. "However, I think I might be tempted to leave out the tobacco." From what she'd seen thus far, cowboying also involved a great deal of spitting.

"Got a point there," Buck said agreeably.

A not uncomfortable silence settled over the kitchen as the elderly man prepared her breakfast and Jude gazed out the window. It was raining, which meant that she hadn't screwed up the shoot by sleeping late since Zach probably wouldn't have been able to get any outdoor shots, anyway.

"Your family certainly chose a stunningly gorgeous place to settle," she said.

"It's good land. Land that breeds life in the grass and grain. There are mornings when I wake up, come downstairs and look out the window and think about all we O'Neills have been blessed with—our valley, the creek, the meadows and mountains, family, neighbors—and I'm not ashamed to admit that it brings tears to these old eyes."

"I can understand that." She'd certainly been more emotional than usual since arriving here.

"There was this one Sunday, back when my wife Josie was still alive, that she invited the new reverend over for Sunday dinner. Now, you have to understand that he was a nice young man, but he was a city fella, and this was his first time east of Boston. Which meant that he'd never seen a working ranch before."

He took some strips of bacon from the warming oven, put them on a plate beside the stack of golden silver dollar pancakes, then placed the plate in front of her, along with a pitcher of maple syrup.

"Well, he was sittin' at that very table, looking out the window at the fields of grass and meadows," he continued. "'My goodness,' I recollect him saying, 'you

O'Neills and the good Lord have certainly created a lovely place up here.'

"Well, I couldn't help myself. I told him, 'Yeah, but it sure took a lot of our hard work to make the good Lord's land fit for ranching.'" He chuckled as Jude laughed. "Josie dang near killed me for that one."

"I can see why she might be a bit peeved," Jude said. "Since he was a guest, and the new minister, at that. But it's still a great story."

"What's a great story?" a deep, familiar voice behind her asked. Jude glanced back over her shoulder and saw Lucky standing in the doorway, looking as if he'd just stepped out of the movie *Silverado* in his black rain duster.

"Buck was telling me about the time the minister came to dinner."

"That is a fair-to-middlin' story." He pulled up a chair, turned it around and straddled it. "So, did he tell you the ending?"

"There's no point in boring the gal," Buck said quickly. Too quickly, Jude thought.

"Actually, I've always thought that was the funniest part." Lucky plucked a piece of the bacon from her plate.

"You always did have a cockeyed sense of humor," the older man grumbled. "Never have figgered out where it came from. You sure as shootin' didn't get it from me."

"So, how did it end?" Jude asked.

"With Buck spendin' that night sleepin' out in the bunkhouse with the hands. He also felt obliged to put a new roof on the church housing the reverend had just moved into."

"The old one leaked like a rusty sieve," Buck grumbled.

"And had every time it rained for the two years prior to that, yet you'd never felt moved to make such a generous donation before." Lucky's eyes danced with the easy humor that Jude found so appealing.

"Your grandmother could be a hard woman, sometimes," Buck said. "But there wasn't a day that went by that I didn't thank God for putting her on this green earth."

"That's so sweet."

Heaven help her, Jude was beginning to feel all weepy again. She really was going to have to take a long vacation once she'd put the *Hunk* special issue to bed. Perhaps somewhere warm and tropical, where she could spend her days lying on a beach beside a tropical lagoon, being waited on hand and foot by handsome beach boys who lived only to please.

"I've always thought so." Lucky's eyes narrowed as they settled on her face. "The O'Neill men have always had good taste in land, horseflesh and women."

When she felt the now familiar sensation of color rising in her cheeks, Jude turned her attention to her breakfast and didn't answer.

THEY BEGAN SHOOTING that afternoon, once Zach proclaimed the golden light that had been washed by the rain perfect. The waving fields of grass, the leaves of the rosebushes planted next to the front door, the fences, even the horses grazing in the pasture all seemed washed by that shimmering soft glow.

"That hat's all wrong," Jude complained as she went over to adjust the felt brim of Lucky's gray Stetson lower over his eyes.

"Pull that down any further and you're going to start casting shadows," Zach warned.

"It's a ridiculous idea anyway," Lucky grumbled from the stock tank he was sitting in. Although they'd let him keep on his underwear, he couldn't recall a time he'd felt more foolish. "Though a cowboy might be forced to take a bath in a stock tank—perhaps if he'd been out on the trail for a long time—I guarantee you, he wouldn't be wearing his dress Sunday hat."

"Creative license," Jude argued wearily.

"It's damn ridiculous," Lucky repeated.

"Stop sulking and it'll be over sooner." She leaned forward and adjusted his pose. As her hair brushed against his cheek, Lucky inhaled her sunshine scent, and immediately felt himself turn as rigid as the trunk of a jack pine. Suddenly he was grateful for the silly froth of bubbles she'd insisted on.

"I'm not sulking." But of course that was exactly what he was doing. "And if you think it's so damn easy, why don't you just climb on in here with me?"

"Perhaps I'll take a rain check," she said instead.

He smiled—with those wonderful lips she imagined she could still taste and his warm dark eyes. "Perhaps I'll just hold you to that," he murmured in a way that made desire thrum through her.

As if they both remembered their reasons for wanting the business side of their relationship over with as soon as possible, Lucky quit arguing over every little thing and began following instructions. He showed a flair that, while not exactly professional, only made him more appealing. And he certainly came off as more real than any pretend cowboy could have, Jude considered as she looked at him, lying back in the sun-dappled hayloft, using his saddle for a pillow, a stick of straw stuck in the corner of his mouth. He was wearing his jeans, the flashy championship buckle, boots, and this time a black hat that gave him a rakish, dangerous look.

"Do you want me to airbrush those scars out?" Zach asked after she'd adjusted the silver screens he was using to bounce the light off Lucky's chest in a way Jude knew would make every subscriber's mouth water.

"No." The white lines bisecting his shoulder, and cutting across his rib cage—additional trophies of his rodeo days, she guessed—only added to his cowboy appeal. "Leave them in."

He grinned. "Good call."

She smiled back. "Thanks."

That was, after all, why she was managing editor of *Hunk of the Month*. At least for now. And from the dynamite shots they'd gotten so far, she knew that the job would be hers for as long as she wanted.

By the time the late summer sun had set, Zach had shot Lucky in the stock tank, the hayloft and astride his mare, his bare chest gleaming with fake sweat that was a combination of baby oil, glycerin and water. They'd also photographed him lying in the pasture, his straw Resitol over his face, appearing to be dozing in a field of blue lupines and yellow-faced daisies that made him seem even more ruggedly masculine by comparison. As she watched Zach snap the shots, Jude came up with the caption: Dreaming of that special cowgirl.

And what woman wouldn't give up manicures and salon cuts for the rest of her life to play that role?

"Thank you," she told Lucky as he used a hose and a bar of Lava soap to get rid of the baby oil, before going back into the house for supper.

Since Zach was losing the light, they'd decided to

shoot the rest of the layout tomorrow, weather permitting. Jude still wanted to get him in the creek—wet, of course—and she thought a shot of him striding across the paddock carrying a bale of hay on his shoulder might be nice, as well. Along with perhaps another one of him pretending to work on the green John Deere tractor.

"You were a good sport."

He shrugged. "So far it hasn't been as bad as I thought it was going to be. Although I sure hate to think what'll happen if Buck ever gets a hold of a copy of that magazine."

"What are you going to tell him?"

"I don't know." He took the towel she handed him and began drying his chest in a way that had her almost swallowing her tongue. The photo shoot, designed to stimulate female fantasies, had definitely stirred her own erotic imagination. "Maybe I can tell him that the X-ray machine at the airport ruined the film."

"That would be a lie." She remembered, all too well, his reaction when he'd learned his sister had lied.

"Nothing like having to eat your own words," he muttered, revealing that they were, once again, thinking the same thing. "They tend to go down hard and dry. Like balls of sawdust."

She'd been so wrapped up in her own concerns— saving the issue, topping Tycoon Mary—that Jude honestly hadn't taken time to consider exactly how all this might impact on Lucky's life. Cremation Creek was a small, isolated community. But she suspected that he wouldn't be able to keep his layout a secret.

Someone—perhaps Dixie or her sister Lila—would undoubtedly run across a copy of the magazine while shopping at the Wal-Mart in Cheyenne and pretty soon he would end up being razzed by his own cowhands. Not to mention having every woman in western Wyoming showing up at the Double Ought. Which might not be a negative to him, but certainly didn't please her.

"I'm sorry." Her eyes backed up the sincerity in her quiet voice. "I should have thought about the attention this will undoubtedly get you." Most men would be flattered to be chosen to be featured as a hunk in her magazine. Even the Philadelphia pipe fitter had ended up signing with a Madison Avenue agency. Jude realized that in this, too, Lucky was an exception.

"It'll blow over."

But in the meantime, Jude thought with a sinking heart, when the issue came out, Lucky was going to feel as if he were riding a whirlwind.

She continued to feel guilty all during supper. And still later, when Lucky went outside to feed the horses. She was upstairs in the pink-and-white wedding cake of a bedroom, working on some papers that Kate had sent via courier, when a tap on the door frame had her looking up to see Lucky standing there.

"I didn't mean to bother you."

"You're not." For the first time in her life she realized that the old expression about a heart having wings was absolutely true. "I was just working on 'the proposal of the month' column."

"Proposal?" He entered the room with that lazy walk that never failed to turn her on. If she'd thought the contrast between the wildflowers and this man was riveting, seeing him here amidst this excess of femininity was enough to make her go so weak at the knees she was grateful she was already sitting on the canopied bed.

"I told you *Hunk of the Month* has more than just beefcake photos. Every month we feature a guest column written by one of our readers...an essay about various topics—the most romantic date, vacation, proposal." She held up the sheets of paper Kate had forwarded. "This one's a proposal.

"So, I guess you have a lot of work to catch up on, having been away from the office, and all."

She was literally drowning in it. There were still at least half a dozen manila folders she hadn't even opened yet. "Not that much."

His lips quirked in a ghost of a smile that told her he knew she was lying. "It's a gorgeous night," he said. "I thought maybe you might like to go for a ride."

"It sounds wonderful, but isn't it kind of dark for horseback riding?"

"I was thinking in my truck. Admittedly, it's not so romantic as a horseback ride, but I figured we could look at some stars and swap life stories like we were talking about doing."

"That sounds perfect." She put away the papers without a second thought.

As she walked with Lucky down the stairs and out of the house, it occurred to Jude that turning her back on work was something the pre-Wyoming, control-addicted managing editor never would have been able to do.

Was it possible for someone to change so much in so short a time? she wondered, vowing to think about this later.

Right now, she was going to enjoy the cool stillness of the Wyoming night. And the company.

11

IT WAS THE KIND of night, Jude thought fancifully, that brought to mind the scene in all the old black-and-white movies in which the handsome cowboy would croon a romantic ballad to a cowgirl. As he drove along the back roads of the ranch, they could have been the only two people in Wyoming. In the world.

"I could get used to this," she murmured, not realizing she'd said the unbidden thought out loud until he glanced over at her.

"Moonlight drives?"

"No. Well, actually, it's nice, too. But I was thinking about the solitude."

"I would have guessed you'd be dying to get back to the hustle and bustle of the city. The bright lights, the fast pace, the crowds, the subway—"

"Not that," she said with a faint, self-conscious laugh, wishing she hadn't brought the subject up. It was difficult to explain what she couldn't quite understand herself. "When I first saw it, from the plane, I thought this looked like about the loneliest place in the world. But I'm beginning to understand how a person can feel separated. But not isolated. Alone, without really being lonely."

He pulled up alongside the creek and cut the engine. When he'd unfastened his seat belt, he draped his wrists over the steering wheel and gave her another long look.

"That's the way I've always felt," he admitted. "But then again, I was born right here on the ranch. I grew up on this land, so what others might find a remote life-style just seems normal to me."

"Did you always feel that way?" She unfastened her own belt, which allowed her to turn sideways so she could look directly up at him. "As if you belonged here?"

"Absolutely. By the time I was five, I'd learned the lesson that Buck—and my daddy—tried to teach me, that the land doesn't belong to us, we belong to the land. And each generation of O'Neills doesn't really inherit the Double Ought, we merely hold it in trust for our grandchildren."

"I like that." She pictured children—a boy and a girl—with their father's Bambi brown eyes and thick dark hair streaked by the unrelenting western sun. "So, there wasn't ever any question about you working on the ranch?"

"Not a one. But not because I felt pressured. If I'd had a yen for city life, no one would have tried to hold me back," he said firmly, making Jude once again wonder if Kate ever regretted her decision to move east. "But I always knew, deep in the bone, I was born to be a cowboy. And a rancher." He looked out over the rolling land that his family had worked and tended for so many generations. "I never, not once, thought of anything else in all my life. I was driving that old John Deere tractor you want to photograph me fixin' by the time I was six.

"Buck and my mama and daddy taught me how to

live right, not to get into fights with our neighbors, and the importance of hard work."

He shook his head and turned toward her. "I feel sorry for the man who has to spend his life doing something he doesn't love. A man who loves his job never has to go to work. At least that's the way I see it."

His somewhat sheepish smile flashed white in the well of darkness surrounding them. "How about you? Did you always want to be a hotshot publishing whiz?"

"I always wanted to publish a magazine. There's something exciting about being in a diner, or the airport, or the subway, and seeing someone enjoying what you do."

"Women read *Hunk of the Month* on the subway?" Right out in public, where anyone can see them? Jude heard his unspoken question.

"Some women. You have to remember, New York's more anonymous than Cremation Creek. No one is going to rush home and tell your mother that you were ogling naked men."

"Near-naked men."

"Near-naked," she agreed with a faint, reminiscent smile as his correction brought back the little skirmish they'd had today over whether or not to photograph him from the back clad solely in his fringed leather chaps. It had been one battle Jude had reluctantly let him win.

"Of course I didn't imagine that I'd edit a magazine exactly like *Hunk of the Month* back when I was a little girl—"

"That was probably a relief to your mom." He'd no sooner said the words than Lucky wished he could recall them. "Hell," he muttered, "I'm sorry, Jude. I forgot about you losing your mother."

"That's all right. It was a long time ago. I've gotten over it." Except when I hear a siren, she thought. Or catch a whiff of smoke.

"How did it happen? Was she sick? Or did she have an accident?"

"It was Christmas Eve." Jude had never told the story to anyone. Her father, who believed in the power of inner strength, had encouraged her to swallow her grief and fear and move on. And she mostly had, except for those occasional flashes of memory that still possessed the power to chill her blood and make her feel five years old again. "We'd all gone to bed, but I'd sneaked downstairs again and was hiding behind my father's chair, hoping to catch a glimpse of Santa Claus."

"I can remember doin' the same thing," Lucky told her. "But I camped out on the roof."

"In December?" It was a wonder he hadn't frozen to death.

He slipped an arm around her in that same easy gesture he had that first night. Just as it had when they'd been sitting on the swing out on the front porch, the light touch of his hand on her shoulder caused her heart to skip a beat.

"I didn't say I stayed out there very long," he said with a quick grin that gave her a very good idea of what this man must have looked like when he was five years old.

It was amazing that he'd grown up to be so responsible, since Jude knew that she, for one, would have difficulty disciplining a child who possessed such a winning smile. The kind of smile designed to coax females of all ages out of warm cookies or the keys to the truck. And, in later years, she had no doubt he used the sensual talent to coax women into bed.

"So." His voice broke into her thoughts, which were threatening to turn erotic on her yet again. "You were telling me about the night you lost your mama."

It was too beautiful a night for this. Tailor-made for romance, not sad memories. "I don't understand what this has to do with what we're doing out here."

"What we're supposed to be doin' out here is getting to know each other," he reminded her.

"I suppose that is what we agreed to." She remembered discussing that, but when he'd invited her on this drive tonight, she'd had a much different scenario in mind.

"Before we get naked," he reminded her.

She laughed and shook her head. "You truly are the most straight-talking man I've ever met."

"I told you, darlin', what you see is pretty much what you get."

And what she'd seen thus far was glorious. "There isn't all that much to tell," she murmured. "I fell asleep, of course. But there was a short in the wiring of the outdoor lights, which started a fire on the roof. My father managed to find me in time to get me out of the house. But my mother died of smoke inhalation."

At least that's what they'd always told her. And coward that she was, she'd never dared press for any more information.

"That's rough." His wide hand soothed her shoulder, his cheek was on the top of her head.

"It does tend to make me more than a bit ambivalent toward Christmas," she admitted.

"You need to spend one here. We'd keep you so

busy climbing all over our mountain, looking for the perfect Christmas tree, and eating Buck's cookies—"

"Buck makes Christmas cookies?"

"The man's a regular Julia Child. Or Keebler elf."

"I wouldn't advise calling him that last name to his face."

"Good idea." His laugh exploded from him, expelling the potentially depressing mood that had threatened. "So, what about your dad?"

"He died last year. On the golf course."

"Although it's too bad for you, it probably wasn't such a bad way to go," Lucky suggested. "Doing what he liked."

"I suppose not." She decided not to contradict him by saying that everyone who ever knew John Lancaster would have expected him to go out while sitting behind his desk, barking orders. Which was, she'd often thought, what he really liked to do best.

She sighed. Lucky sighed.

"I guess this wasn't the best idea after all," he said.

"No. It was a great idea." She turned toward him, surprised to find that their faces were so close together. All she'd have to do to kiss him would be to lean forward the least little bit....

"Favorite ice cream," he said suddenly, shattering yet another sensual fantasy.

"Butter pecan," she answered off the top of her head. "How about you?"

"Vanilla."

She was not surprised.

"With chocolate sauce."

The way he was looking at her, his eyes gleaming as if she were a hot fudge sundae made Jude tingle all the way to her toes.

Determined to take things slowly, to get to know her before ripping the clothes off that trim little body, Lucky stomped down the image of pouring Hershey's sauce all over Jude, then licking it off.

"Favorite vacation spot," he said. "Mountains or the beach?"

"The mountains," she answered promptly, not adding that until recently she would have chosen the beach. Every beach boy, pirate, tropical lagoon fantasy she'd ever indulged in paled in comparison to the idea of making love to Lucky in some high country meadow. Or one of the natural hot springs Zach had told her about while they'd been rounding up the bulls.

"Mine, too, which probably doesn't make a lick of sense, since I already live in them. But I've never been all that fond of sand. It can get in some really uncomfortable places, if you know what I mean."

Oh, she most definitely did. Especially since she was currently vividly aware of those particular places which were feeling more and more uncomfortably hot.

"Favorite movie."

"I suppose that's a four-way tie. Anything with Tom Cruise. *While You Were Sleeping. Sleepless in Seattle.* And *Ghost.*"

"Ah, the high-powered career lady is a closet romantic."

She tossed her head. "Something wrong with romance?"

"Nothing at all."

His gaze was warm enough to melt her into a puddle of desire on the floor of his pickup cab. "How about yours?"

"How about my what?" He was looking at her

mouth. Jude thought if he didn't kiss her soon, she'd have to throw herself at him.

"Favorite movie."

"Oh." He seemed to have lost interest in the conversation. "*Young Guns. Comes a Horseman.* Oh, and *Old Yeller.*"

"The one about the dog getting rabies?"

"That's it. Every time I see that movie, I bawl my eyes out." His gaze, which had been centered on her lips, moved upward to her eyes. "Guess I shouldn't have told you that.... You'll probably think I'm a big old sissy."

"No one could ever think that." She touched her fingers to his cheek, felt a muscle clench, and knew that he was no less affected by the tension that was strung between them as tight as barbwire.

He cupped her chin in his hand; his thumb brushed against her lips. "Jude—"

"Yes." Her lips parted at the softly stroking touch, the single word expelled on a breath of warm need.

He needed no further invitation. His mouth captured hers, crushing, conquering, as he pulled her onto his lap and held her tight against him.

His teeth, scraping over her lower lip, dazed. His mouth, as it drank deeply, insistently from hers, stole the very breath from her lungs. The passion that had been simmering beneath the surface since that shared kiss in the barn sparked like a Wyoming wildfire. Jude gasped as he tugged her shirt free of her waistband and shoved his hands beneath it, his fingers digging into her waist as he rotated her hips against the huge hard bulge in his loins. Control shattered, Jude clung to his shoulders, willing to go wherever he took her, eager to ride him all night long as he began touching her, stroking her, wherever he could reach.

A ragged curse felt like a hot wind against her mouth as he struggled with the catch of her bra. He tore at it in the same way he'd torn at her self-control from that first meeting, ripping it away.

He cupped her breasts in those wide dark hands she'd seen wield a rope with unerring accuracy. His callused thumbs rasped against her ultrasensitive nipples like sandpaper, wrenching an involuntary whimper from her ravished lips.

She could have screamed when he suddenly stopped the painfully pleasurable caress. "Did I hurt you?"

"No." Desperate, she arched against him. "Never." Her avid mouth ate into his. She ripped open his shirt, as she had in the barn. "I need…" She pressed her open mouth against his rib cage. "I want…" Her voice drifted off as the dark male taste emanating from his hot damp flesh intoxicated her.

"Sweet heaven." Lucky moaned and tore at her belt, gaining access to the metal button at her waist. Displaying the strength that allowed him to control a thousand pounds of horse and chase down a ton of bull, he lifted her up with one hand, while yanking the zipper down with the other. "I want you, too, darlin'. All of you."

His touch was profoundly intimate and possessive. His fingers delved deep, then deeper still, pushing her closer and closer to the edge, claiming every ounce of her control, claiming her in a primal way that went beyond the physical. And even as she struggled to maintain some ragged grasp on sanity, he touched her sensitive bud with his thumb, a swift, practiced stroke that sent a series of convulsions ripping through her.

Jude cried out and would have pulled away, but he refused to release her, holding her tight, his arm locked around her like an iron band, as he wrenched climax after shuddering climax from the body she no longer controlled. Just when she was certain she had no more to give, he proved her wrong. He swallowed her strangled cry, kissing her until the storm had passed.

She had no idea how long she lay there, limp and exhausted in his arms, gasping for breath. It was as if having spun out of its axis, the planet had now ceased spinning altogether.

"Do you have any idea what you do to me?" The blood was still pounding thickly in her ears, making his deep voice sound as if it were coming from far away. His hand still cupped her intimately, but with tenderness now, rather than passion. "How you make me feel?"

As Jude struggled to focus on the meaning of his words she felt the unmistakable proof of his still unsatiated arousal beneath her bottom and belatedly realized how selfish she'd been.

"I'm sorry. It's your turn—"

As she turned her attention to his gleaming silver buckle, he forestalled her, holding both her wrists with one hand.

"That's not what I mean.... Well, perhaps it is," he admitted, as his body swelled even harder in anticipation of the sweet touch he seemed determined not to allow. As his deep chuckle vibrated through her, Jude thought it said a great deal about Lucky O'Neill's character that he could find humor in this situation. "What

I meant was, do you realize the number you do on my self-control?"

"*Your* self-control?" If she'd had the energy left, she would have laughed at that. "You're not exactly the one turned inside out here, cowboy."

Her heart did a little stutter step as he treated her to another of those dazzling grins that she'd come to realize made him the irresistible man he was even more than his thick hair and muscle-roped arms.

"Is that a compliment I hear coming from those tender, petal pink lips, New York?"

"Of course it is." She smiled back, wondering why it was that she, who had always managed to avoid talking about sex in the past, even afterward—*especially* afterward—felt so comfortable now. "I realize you'll probably think this is a horrendous cliché, but I never knew I could have more than one...well..." So much for feeling comfortable. As Jude felt the heat flood into her face, she was grateful for the darkness. "You know."

"Yeah." He touched his smiling lips to hers. "I know."

The kiss started out soft, but as he slowly deepened it, degree by devastating degree, Jude was stunned to feel a renewed stir of desire.

"I want you," she murmured raggedly as his lips plucked at hers and his fingers began making sensual little figure eights through the silky hair at the juncture of her thighs, which were beginning to tremble all over again.

"Aw sweetheart, I want you, too." He parted the soft swollen flesh, dipped a finger into her wet warmth and drew a shimmering sound that was half sigh, half moan.

"Not that way," Jude said, even as her rebellious body—which definitely had a mind of its own—arched against the intimate touch. "I want you inside me. All of you."

"I want that, too," he repeated. Then cursed, released her lips and rested his forehead against hers. "But the thing is, darlin', I really didn't plan for this."

"That's all right." She drew away, framed his atypically somber face between her palms and bestowed her sweetest, most seductive smile upon him. "Some of the best things in life are spontaneous."

With desire thrumming anew through her veins, Jude wasn't about to admit that she couldn't recall the last time she'd done anything spontaneous. Other than follow Lucky to Wyoming, she considered on an afterthought. And look how lovely that had turned out.

"The point is...dammit," he cursed again through clenched teeth as she stroked her palm across the placket of his jeans. The denim was straining from the heavy male bulge. "The point—and dear Lord, I do have one—" he rasped, "is that I didn't exactly come here tonight prepared to make love to you."

He fisted his hand in her hair, lifted her gaze to his, and sighed heavily. "The way I see it, we have two choices."

"What are they?" If they kept talking much longer, she was going to grasp hold of the reins of control again, yank down that damn zipper and take him in her mouth. The way she'd dreamed last night. Slowly. Deeply...

His next words jerked her from that erotic fantasy.

"We can go back to the Double Ought and I'll drive

into Cremation Creek at first light tomorrow morning and—"

"That's not an option."

"Darlin', I was hoping you'd say that." He put his hands under her arms, lifted her as easily as if she were a feather and deposited her back onto her seat. "Buckle up."

"What?" She stared at him as if he'd suddenly begun speaking a foreign language.

"It's the law. Drivers and passengers have to buckle up when the truck's moving."

"We're moving?" When he started the engine, she did as instructed. "Where are we going?"

"To Cremation Creek."

"Oh, no." She groaned and slumped back onto the seat and told herself she should have seen this one coming. "We're going to the Feed and Fuel for condoms, aren't we?"

His answering grin was filled with admiration and promise and sexy as hell. "I knew you were as smart as a whip, New York."

Knowing that it would do her no earthly good to argue, Jude sat back, gazed out at the wide star-spangled sky and decided, for once in her life, to go with the flow.

12

THE DRIVE TO Johnny Murphy's Feed and Fuel seemed to take forever. Anticipation thrummed in the cab of the pickup, like electricity through a high-voltage wire. There was a thunderstorm in the distance; sulfurous flashes of lightning lit up the horizon along with the dusty red glow of the wildfires that were still burning out of control.

"Do you think the fires will reach us?" she asked.

Now that he knew her family history, Lucky understood the reason for the uncharacteristic nervousness he'd heard in her voice whenever she mentioned the fires.

"Nah," he assured her with more conviction than he felt, as he gave her hand a gentle squeeze. "The wind's blowing the wrong way."

"But it could change."

"True. But we'd have plenty of warning, Jude." He lifted her hand to his lips and brushed a light kiss against her knuckles. "There's nothing to worry about."

She desperately wished she could believe him. But old fears, it seemed, ran deep. "It would be such a shame," she murmured, "if your hay would burn up before you could get it in." He'd told her that next week he was planning to begin cutting the native wheat grass hay they used to feed the cows during the long cold winters.

"We'd just have to buy some off Johnny, or some other rancher," he said. Such a nonchalant attitude, she guessed, was necessary to a man who depended on the vagaries of nature. "Thanks to you and your hunk magazine, we'll have enough money to buy all we may need."

"It really is going to be a terrific issue, Lucky. I knew you were going to look sexy, but believe me, you're going to be our best hunk yet."

He laughed to hide his embarrassment. Although as the day had gone by, he'd begun to relax just a little— thanks in part to Zach Newman's casual, matter-of-fact work attitude—the idea of an O'Neill man posing for such a magazine still proved more than a little discomfiting.

"If I look sexy, it's because of you."

"Me?"

"Because of what I'm thinking. Because I look over at you and imagine all the things I want to do to you. With you." He turned their still-joined hands and touched the tip of his tongue to the center of her palm, creating an instantaneous spark of heat she imagined she could hear sizzling in the stillness of the night. "Of all the things I want you to do to me. With me."

"I know." She'd seen the lust in his gaze as he'd looked up at her from his bed of wildflowers in the meadow, felt his hunger as she'd leaned over the stock tank to arrange the frothy bubbles. "I've been thinking all those things. And more." Her voice was soft and faint, as if coming from one of the sensual dreams she'd been suffering while tossing and turning in Kate's teenage bed.

"I'd kind of hoped I could stick to the deal we'd made," he admitted. "Waiting until we'd gotten the work out of the way."

"We're almost done. Zach only has a few more shots to take tomorrow."

"Then you go back to New York."

"Yes." Her tone was as flat as his when she thought of leaving the Double Ought. And him. "But, you know, now that I think about it, the rest of the magazine is already done. All that was left was the cowboy hunk. Which, thanks to you, I now have."

She crossed her legs, then recrossed them, suddenly nervous about making the suggestion. "I was thinking perhaps I could take a few days off."

"At the Double Ought?"

"If it's all right with you. I mean, I understand that you and Buck aren't running a dude ranch, and you haven't really invited me to stay, but—"

"Jude." He leaned over and pressed a quick hard kiss against her lips to shut her up. And even though she found his method of cutting off her words chauvinistic, she couldn't deny that the touch of his mouth on hers still had the power to rock her to her toes. "There's nothing I'd like better than to have you stay on here with me. For as long as you'd like."

"Well." She smiled and wondered what he'd do if she just called Kate and had her ship everything she owned out to the Double Ought. Unfortunately, her life—and any serious opportunity to work in publishing—was back in Manhattan. "Although I can't stay as long as I'd like, Kate can probably hold down the fort for another three or four days."

It wasn't much, Lucky thought. Not when he'd prefer a lifetime. However, not being one to look a gift horse in the mouth, he decided to be grateful for however long he could keep this woman in Wyoming. With him.

From the number of pickups in the parking lot at the Feed and Fuel, it appeared half the county had decided to show up at the store tonight. While Lucky went inside—he didn't invite Jude to join him and she certainly wasn't about to volunteer—she waited in the truck, reading the various bumper stickers. I Brake For Good Looking Cowboys, one warned. Another, advertising a Laramie steak house, stated that Pasta Isn't A Main Dish At Any Meal. A third warned, Always Drink Upstream From The Herd. And yet a fourth proclaimed something Jude had already concluded during her brief time in the west: You Can Take the Cowboy Out of the Country, But You Can't Take the Country Out of the Cowboy.

Even if Lucky hadn't told her about growing up knowing he belonged here in cowboy country, she couldn't have been able to imagine him living anywhere else other than Wyoming. Cowboy life had a hold on the man. With a long, strong rope. And she couldn't imagine him ever doing anything else.

Which meant, of course, that there was no future in their relationship. Because even if she wanted to stay here with him—and a very large part of her was sorely tempted to do exactly that—she knew that she'd never be happy as a traditional ranch wife. And even if she could settle down and spend her days cooking enormous quantities of chicken-fried steak, beef, country-fried potatoes and homemade bread, there was always the little fact that her culinary skills consisted of nuking diet dinners in the microwave or opening a can of soup. There was no way she could compete with Buck in the kitchen, even if she wanted to. Which she didn't.

But she did want Lucky O'Neill, dammit. With a passion that frightened her. And made her almost a stranger to herself.

She was so caught up in trying to understand these atypical feelings that she failed to see Lucky return. She literally jumped when he opened the driver's door of the Dodge.

"You looked about a million miles away." He was smiling, but in the glow of the mercury vapor floodlight illuminating the parking lot, she could see the seeds of concern in his midnight dark eyes.

"I was just thinking."

"Must not have been all that pretty a thought." He put the key in the ignition and twisted it, bringing the massive engine under the cherry red hood to life. "If you're trying to figure out how to tell me you've changed your mind—"

"No." She put her hand on his thigh as he pulled out of the parking lot and headed back toward the Double Ought. "I was just thinking about possibilities," she admitted wistfully.

"Isn't that a coincidence. Because where you are concerned, little darlin', that's just about all I've been pondering lately myself."

Jude didn't even consider challenging him on calling her "little darlin'." Not only did she know it wouldn't do any good, she also had to admit that, deep down inside, it made her feel feminine. And desirable.

He drove back to that same place beside the creek, and wasted no time hauling her from her seat into his arms. He began kissing her in a way that made her head spin and wiped her mind as clear as polished glass.

Jude kissed him back, deeply, hungrily. She twined her arms around the strong tanned column of his neck and clung to him, her body hot and pliant. And needy.

He was breathing hard; his chest was heaving up and down like a bellows.

"Lucky..." A moan caught at the back of her throat. Urgency had her twisting in his arms as his rough strong hands moved over her, from her shoulders to her thighs, kneading her scorching flesh, cupping her swollen breasts, rubbing hard at the denim between her legs. "Please..."

The only thing she'd had to drink tonight was Buck's horseshoe-melting coffee, and yet she felt drunk. Drunk with desire. With need. Although the steering wheel was hard against her back, as she straddled him, arching in a way that begged him to take her breasts in his mouth, she was only dimly aware of a vague discomfort.

He caught hold of the V-neck of the blue-and-white plaid shirt and yanked it open, sending buttons flying. They scattered onto the floor mat, the white plastic gleaming like pearls in the moonlight streaming through the windshield. An animal growl rumbled deep in his throat as he took the offered flesh in his mouth, suckling deeply, not as a child, but as a man would. A man who could make her weak with a single look, her heart sing from a flash of a cocky cowboy grin, her entire body ache from the touch of those work-roughened hands.

She tangled her hands in his hair, pushing him deeper into her yielding flesh, spread her legs wider, rubbing against his rock-hard erection. The sound of denim rasping against denim sounded unnaturally loud in the cramped confines of the pickup cab.

"If we keep this up, I'm going to explode like some horny teenage kid," he groaned, burying his mouth in the fragrant curve of her neck. His body was already racing toward the finish line, and his heart was beating so hard and so fast in his chest, Lucky wondered if it was possible to be having a damn heart attack at his age. "I want you, Jude. But not this way, wrestling in the front seat of a truck. I want to lie with you, naked, flesh to flesh, man to woman, like the good Lord intended."

An errant thought flashed unbidden through her mind. A thought Jude instantly tamped down. No way was she going to suggest that the good Lord to whom Lucky referred undoubtedly would have preferred them to be married before they started joining that hot male and female flesh.

"I want that, too." More than she could say. "But where—"

"Boy Scouts aren't the only ones who come prepared." He grinned and kissed away her frown. "I might have forgotten the overcoat. But there's a bedroll in the back of the truck."

She laughed. Then kissed him deeper. Harder. "My hero," she sighed.

Later she would realize she had no idea how, exactly, she got from sitting in the front seat to lying on the sleeping bag beneath the endless glittering sky. But however he'd managed it, Jude knew that it was a night she'd remember for the rest of her life.

Lucky wanted to take things slow. To do them right. That had been his intention, during the earlier makeout session, and while he'd been buying the rubbers that had let Johnny, Dixie, and seemingly half the cowboys in the county who'd gathered in the store, know his plans for the night. It was a vow he'd repeated to himself over and over again on the drive back to this spot that had always held so many fond teenage memories, but from now on would only remind him of this woman.

But he hadn't counted on her hands stoking such hot internal fires so fast, hadn't planned on her scent drawing him like a bee to a honeycomb. And he definitely hadn't expected the panic that set in when he realized that somehow, when he hadn't been paying proper attention, he'd fallen in love with this sweet-smelling city slicker.

The knowledge that this would probably be all they'd ever have, that she'd be gone in another few days, taking his heart back east with her, caused the last tether on his control to unravel.

They were lying side by side, one of her hands playing with his hair, the other stroking his length in a slow, sensual rhythm that had him swell beneath her touch. Need overcame his fear of losing her, and Lucky rolled her over in one swift movement, covering her damp slick body with his.

"I want you." He thrust her legs apart, not gently. "Now." *Forever*, he thought grimly.

"Now." *Always*, she wished silently.

And then, with intimate secrets hovering thickly in the air between them, he drove into her with a deep, battering force that made her cry out.

"Oh, yes," she gasped before he could ask if he'd hurt her. Her fingernails etched anxious, needy paths up and down his back. "Don't stop." She grasped hold of his taut buttocks, pulling him tighter against her.

"Whatever you do, don't—" she was panting, already breathless "—ever stop."

"That might be beyond even my capabilities," he managed to reply in a strangled tone. "But since I don't want it said I ever disappointed a lady, I'll give it a shot."

He braced himself on his forearms and began moving against her, slowly, rhythmically, his eyes on hers, holding her gaze with the steely strength of his will as he drove her into the softness of the bedroll, then pulled nearly all the way out again, going deeper and deeper with each successive thrust.

"Put your legs around my hips, darlin'. So you can take all of me."

She'd been afraid that was going to be impossible. But she did as instructed, and he sank deeper still, until his groin was rubbing against acutely sensitive tissues, causing a climax like sparklers on the Fourth of July.

"That's my girl."

He touched his mouth to hers, his tongue echoing the invasion of his shaft as he sank back into her, this time all the way to the hilt. When she felt him touch the back of her womb, she came again, this time with a rush of feeling that felt like waves crashing against the shore.

The hot flood of her release was all it took to trigger Lucky's own. His entire body tensed—arms, shoulders, back, thighs. The muscles in his neck corded and, as the pressure built like a branding iron at the base of his spine, his hips began pumping, harder, faster. His groans rumbled in the dark of night like wild animal growls.

He felt her come again, her inner convulsions clutching at him, massaging him in a way that caused a wrenching climax to rip through him. Then he collapsed on top of her, the sound of her name that had been torn from his throat at the moment of release lingering on the night breeze.

Afraid he was crushing her, he rolled over, taking her with him, staying inside her when she managed a murmured plea for him not to leave. As they lay in each other's arms, their heated flesh cooling, Lucky stared up at the diamond bright sky and wondered what the hell he'd gotten himself into. And why, as Jude snuggled closer, murmuring soft inarticulate words of pleasure, he was considering getting out his rope and tying her to the truck. To the Double Ought. To him.

He was actually allowing himself to contemplate somehow working out a long-distance relationship with this city slicker. But he had to face that she'd irretrievably slipped beneath his skin and trespassed into his heart.

Suddenly he felt her lips trembling against his chest. And the way her shoulders were shaking revealed she was weeping.

Terrific. *Make the lady cry, O'Neill,* he blasted himself.

"Jude?" He caught her chin and lifted her gaze to his. "Sweetheart? Did I hurt you?"

"No." She bit her trembling lip. "I was just—um—thinking about something."

He wondered if she was crying about having to go back east to her magazine and, although he knew it was selfish as hell, Lucky kind of wished she was.

"Care to share?" Her eyes were bright and wet. He braced himself for an onslaught of female tears.

"I just realized..." She took a ragged breath. "I just finally figured out why it's called a pickup *bed.*"

He chuckled even as he felt chagrined that he hadn't used more finesse the first time. "You deserve better."

She touched her hand to his cheek, her look as warm as the maple syrup Buck heated up on Sunday mornings for flapjacks. "I can't imagine topping that."

Masculine pride warred with the tenderness she seemed to inspire. "You're probably used to soft music—"

"We have the breeze in the tops of the trees," she said with a soft smile that seemed strangely shy, considering what they'd just shared.

"Champagne."

"I already feel drunk enough whenever you kiss me."

"Satin sheets."

"Too slippery." She wiggled against him with the obvious intention of rekindling smoldering sparks. "I can't think of anywhere else I'd rather be right now. Any other man I'd rather be with."

The way she was moving had desire pounding in his loins. He couldn't seem to be with Jude and not want her. More terrifyingly yet, not need her.

He pulled her on top of him, fitting her soft curves to his hard angles. "I want you again."

The feel of him, hard and urgent beneath her, was all it took to send anticipation soaring. "I want you, too."

She bent down, her lips plucking at his, the ruby hard tips of her breasts brushing against his bare chest. Although she'd been looking at his near-naked body all day, it still drew her like a lodestone.

Proving that with the right incentive she could proceed slowly, Jude slid down him, pressing lingering kisses against the chestnut hair that arrowed down the center of his body. She circled his navel with the tip of her tongue and realized the extent of her power when his legs began to shift restlessly beneath hers.

''Jude—''

She laughed, a soft, shimmering sound, enjoying herself. Enjoying him. Lucky O'Neill was a magnificent male animal. And for this one magical night, he was all hers.

She was merciless, tempting, tantalizing, teasing, drawing the exquisite lovemaking out, until they were both strung as taut as a rope around the horns of a stubborn bull. Despite the seeming disparity in their life-styles, in this, at least, they proved perfectly matched. By the time the morning sun spread its shimmering rays over the distant mountaintop, both knew that what they'd experienced during the long love-filled night had been more than mere sex. The profound intimacy they'd shared had surpassed the physical. And inexorably changed their lives.

"We have to talk about it," Lucky said after they'd managed to retrieve the clothes that were scattered in the bed of the truck and the front and back seats.

Since the morning had dawned cool and her shirt was essentially useless due to its lack of buttons, she was wearing his denim jacket. She pulled it tighter and momentarily wished that he wasn't such a plainspoken man. She would have preferred allowing herself to continue basking in the warm pleasurable afterglow. There'd been more than once during the seemingly endless night when she'd actually allowed herself the fantasy of staying in Wyoming with this man—a man who could make her heart sing and her body flame. She wasn't quite ready to deal with the problems of real life.

"What's to talk about?" She prepared herself for him

to tell her all the reasons why any relationship between them wouldn't work out. "It was sex, Lucky. Better than I've ever had before, better than I ever thought possible, but that's all it was."

"Liar." His tone was firm, but lacked heat. "Sex is easy, darlin'. Too easy, sometimes. This was different." He glanced over at her, his expression stone-serious in the shimmering morning light. "You're different."

She couldn't lie. Not about this. "So are you," she said quietly. Then waited—her breath in her throat—for him to ask her to stay here at the Double Ought with him.

"The logical thing would be to just enjoy the next few days and not worry about it."

"I've never been one to go in for vacation flings."

"Me, neither."

"Well...you could ask me to stay."

"No." His fingers tightened on the steering wheel as if the gesture could hold back those very words he was sorely tempted to say. When he felt her flinch, he realized how curt he'd sounded. "That's not my place. You have your own life, New York. An important life. I may be accused of being old-fashioned from time to time, but I'm not such a chauvinist that I'd expect you to give all that up for me."

What would she be giving up? Jude asked herself honestly. A noisy, crowded city, a day spent with jangling phones, computer glitches, Tycoon Mary breathing over her shoulder, a life where her only close friend was this man's sister, where her entire existence revolved around work, where antacids were merely another food group?

"What if I wanted to?" She didn't want to push. But she needed to know exactly how Lucky felt about her.

He plowed his hand through his hair and exhaled a long, frustrated breath. "Maybe you don't indulge in flings, but you've undoubtedly been hit with City Slicker Syndrome. I've seen it before, Jude, people come out here for a couple weeks in the summer, fall in love with the land, envision living like some western novel, with their pretty horses and cute baby cows, without thinking about the fact that they're not going to able to run out to the corner store at midnight for ice cream—"

"Actually, I seldom eat ice cream."

"You know what I mean," he said in a way that had Jude wishing again that the subject hadn't come up.

"Yes. I do." She reached out, caught his hand as it completed another frustrated pass through his hair and linked their fingers together. "It's been a long night. Though a wonderful one," she said quickly when he shot her a look. "But neither of us have had much sleep. Perhaps we'd be better off discussing this later. When we've both had time to gather our thoughts." *And our arguments.*

"Are you trying to manipulate me again, New York?"

His tone lacked an edge, letting her know that he was teasing. "Yes. Is it working?"

"I'll let you know. After I get some sleep."

"That sounds very reasonable."

"I don't know about reasonable. I wasn't exactly thinking of sleeping alone."

Oh. "That sounds better yet."

"Yeah." He gave her hand a quick squeeze. "One more thing we can agree one. Looks as if we're on a roll, darlin'."

ANY THOUGHTS JUDE might have had of inviting Lucky into her bed disintegrated when they pulled up in front of the ranch house. A huge tractor trailer was parked between the house and the barn. O'Neill Rodeo Stock had been written across the gleaming white surface in shamrock green paint.

Lucky didn't sound particularly excited to see the trailer. "My folks are back."

"Oh." Although she was a grown woman, Jude suddenly felt as if she were sixteen years old and about to get caught staying out all night after the prom.

Once again Lucky proved to be on the same wavelength. "Maybe we can sneak in the back way."

They looked at each other as he parked the truck beside the trailer, then burst out laughing at the ridiculousness of their situation.

Marianne O'Neill didn't so much as raise an eyebrow at their disheveled condition. She rose from the kitchen table, greeted her son with a hug, then turned to Jude with a friendly smile.

She was a tall, slender woman who seemed, like Lucky, not to have a superfluous ounce of fat on her. Hard work had muscled her shoulders and arms, the sun had created little lines at the corners of her brown eyes, suggesting she was a woman who smiled easily. And often.

"Hello." She held out a slender hand. "Welcome to our home, Jude. Buck's been telling me all about you."

"Oh, dear." Jude shook the hand that proved stronger than it looked.

Lucky's mother laughed at Jude's feeble attempt at humor. "It's all good, believe me. In fact, we were just discussing your magazine when you came in—"

"Where's Dad?" Lucky interrupted, wanting to

avoid any discussion of *Hunk of the Month*. He may have been able to sidestep Buck, but his mother was another matter entirely. Although outwardly she could appear really easygoing, he also knew she could be like a damn pit bull worrying a bone when she got her teeth sunk into something.

"He's out in the barn, with that nice young man. Your photographer," she told Jude.

"Zach."

"Yes." Marianne smiled again. "I knew his mother. Lovely woman, a champion barrel racer, like her daughter, and her quilts always won the blue ribbon at the county fair. I hadn't seen Zach since he was a young 'un. I should have realized he wasn't a boy any longer, but it did come as a surprise to see that he's all grown up." She sighed. "Just like my own children...

"And speaking of my children...how is Katie? Buck suggested that she was having problems—"

"It was just a misunderstanding, Mom," Lucky assured her quickly. He exchanged a look with Jude. "I think, if you don't mind, I'll go out and say hi to Dad."

"Of course, dear. That will give Jude and me an opportunity to get acquainted."

At that, Lucky shot Jude another questioning look that she answered with a faint nod. She could handle this, she thought, holding the jacket closed. She was, after all, an adult woman with an important, high-powered career. There was no reason to feel uncomfortable just because she'd spent the night rolling around in this woman's son's sleeping bag.

Lucky surprised her, drawing her to him for a quick kiss that rocked her and caused color to darken her cheekbones. "Good luck," he murmured. "And remember, if you need rescuing, the cavalry's just across the way in the barn."

With that single playful statement, he eased her nervousness. Before Jude knew what was happening, she was sitting at the pine table with Lucky's mother, drinking coffee and discussing Kate.

"The boys were worried when she fell in love with Jack," Marianne divulged. "In fact, I had to practically sit on my husband to keep him from going to New York when she moved in with him. I reminded him that, although she'd always be our darling baby girl, Kate was a grown woman. Capable of making her own decisions. Men," she said as she heated up their coffee from a Mr. Coffee carafe Jude hadn't seen before, "can be so terribly old-fashioned. And I'm afraid the O'Neill men in some ways are worse than most."

"So I've discovered." Jude took a sip of the re-warmed coffee. "This is wonderful." She practically wept as she felt the warm rush of caffeine jolt through her.

"Thank you. But of course boiled mud would taste good after Buck's battery acid."

"It is a little strong."

"It's horrendous. We've all hated it for years, but he seems real proud of it, so none of us have had the heart to try to get him to change the recipe."

"You have a wonderful family."

"It's not that unusual. We have our spats, but when you live an isolated life as we do out here, you grow up understanding that, when push comes to shove, family is the one thing you can always count on.

"I'm so pleased we've finally met," she continued, seeming to change the subject. "Kate has told me so much about you. I was sorry to hear that you'd lost your father last year."

"I was sorry, too. But at least he died doing what he loved to do." She'd decided Lucky had a point about that.

"True. My Michael has always insisted that he wants to die in the saddle."

"With his boots on," Jude suggested.

Marianne's laugh was lighter, more musical than her son's, but Jude could see the resemblance in the gleaming brown eyes. "Exactly." She took another longer sip of coffee and eyed Jude thoughtfully over the rim of the mug. "So, I take it my son is going to be your Hunk of the Month."

A blaze of color flamed her cheeks. "You know about the magazine?"

"Of course. I bought a copy as soon as Kate told us you'd hired her as your assistant. It's quite...how should I put this?...stimulating."

"Does your husband know?"

"About Lucky? No, not yet. But I will tell him. We've never kept secrets from one another."

Oh, God. Jude worried how Lucky was going to react to his parents knowing he'd agreed to pose in those bubbles.

"I think he'll be a little surprised," Marianne admitted. "But after the initial shock wears off, I have no doubt he'll view it as I do...as a terrific PR vehicle for the cowboy way."

Jude began to relax. "That's what I told Lucky."

"And aren't you a clever woman?" Marianne beamed at her. "No wonder my son's fallen in love with you."

"Oh, he's not—"

"Of course he is, darling. Trust me, I've watched the girls come and go in my son's life. But the last time I ever saw that gleam that's in his eyes when he looks at you was his sixth Christmas when he came downstairs and discovered the sheltie mix puppy Santa had left him."

"That's quite a comparison," Jude murmured, reaching for one of the biscuits that were in their usual basket in the middle of the table.

"It may seem a bit unflattering," Marianne admitted. "But not if you knew how much he loved that dog. So, how do you feel about him?"

"I don't know." Her gaze slid out the window to where the three O'Neill men were busy unloading horses from the trailer. "Confused, mostly."

"A sure sign."

"It's been such a short time." She looked down at her hands which were trembling ever so slightly. Jude knew how to achieve success in the workplace. Unfortunately, she didn't have a clue how to manage her personal life. She'd tried to convince herself that her feelings for Lucky had been based on lust. But that had been the biggest lie of all. She cared for him. Deeply. Truly. But having been brought up to avoid spontaneity, she couldn't quite trust her unruly feelings now. "We only met a few days ago."

"I knew the minute Lucky's father landed in my medical tent that he was the man for me."

"You were lucky."

"True. But if there's one thing that all the years of ranching has taught me, dear, it's that sometimes we make our own luck."

That stated, Lucky's mother stood up, put her mug in the dishwasher, and headed toward the kitchen door. "I have to go help Michael with the stock," she said. "I hope we'll have many more opportunities for some girl chats. As much as I dearly love my husband, and our life, the rodeo world is overpopulated with males. It's always a treat to get to talk about things like hairstyles and the latest fashion rather than the difference in torque between a Dodge truck or a Chevy, or horse colic, or the best way to control botflies."

"We should finish up shooting today," Jude said. "Then I'd planned to stay for a few more days before returning to Manhattan."

Something flickered in the depths of Lucky's mother's dark eyes, but it came and went too fast for Jude to decode it.

"Isn't that nice?" she said neutrally, then left the kitchen.

Jude watched her walk across the gravel driveway, watched the way Lucky's father put a casual, affectionate arm around her waist, observed the way they seemed to fit so perfectly in each other's space. He bent down and said something, his mouth close to her ear, suggesting his words were just for her.

She smiled up at him and even from this distance, Jude could see her warm and generous heart in her eyes. As he smiled back and brushed a finger down her cheek, in a casually intimate gesture that reminded Jude of his son, emotion welled up in her, moistening her eyes, blurring her vision.

As impossible as it sounded, Jude knew that she'd fallen in love with Lucky. The idea was thrilling and terrifying all at the same time. She'd worked hard to get where she was, struggled to achieve the level of success she enjoyed, proving all those naysayers—who'd thought she'd only been hired because of her father—wrong. But the pleasure she'd once gotten from her work had dulled, like a pretty gold ring that turned out to be brass.

"So you're sick of your job," she murmured. "Join the real world, kiddo." If she was dissatisfied where she was, changing careers was the logical thing to do. And Jude had always prided herself on being a logical, practical woman.

Falling in love with a cowboy from Cremation Creek, Wyoming was not the slightest bit logical. But that was exactly what had happened. The problem was, she wondered as she pushed herself up from the table, could love be enough?

13

THE NEXT FEW DAYS flew by, making a mockery of Jude's attempt to stop the world—or at least their little corner of it—from spinning. Zach finished taking the pictures, proclaimed himself brilliant, overnighted the film back to New York for processing, then took the opportunity of their unscheduled vacation to visit his family on their ranch.

During this time, Kate was calling several times a day with ultimatums and threats from Tycoon Mary, but determined to live for the moment for once in her life, Jude dug in the heels of her boots and refused to budge. She spent every moment she could with Lucky. The two of them rode Lightning and Annie over the meadows and through the woods. They necked in the back row of the balcony of The Gilded Lily while Clint Eastwood's six guns were blazing away in *The Good, the Bad and the Ugly*. She even enjoyed sitting in Lucky's study with him after dinner, watching him work on the ranch books that were now on computer.

He was, she'd come to realize, much more than a "mere cowboy." He seemed to be equal parts ranch manager, accountant, wildlife manager, veterinarian and environmentalist. In fact, Buck had told her proudly, because he'd suspected Lucky wouldn't, last year the ranch had won a national government award for an educational program Lucky had set up allowing students to visit the ranch to study wildlife, streams, vegetation, geology, archaeology, birds and riparian areas. He was so many things, she mused. And amazingly, he was hers.

"You realize, of course," Lucky murmured late in the afternoon of her fourth day of playing hooky, "you're not going to be able to hide out here with me forever."

They were lying in each other's arms, after fulfilling both their fantasies of making love in a hayloft.

"I know." She held him tighter, as if she could prevent their time together from slipping away. "I keep telling myself that. But what if I were just to fax in my resignation?" She held her breath, waiting for the words she longed to hear. The words she'd once promised she would not need.

He plucked a piece of straw from her tangled hair. "You don't want to do that."

"You can be so arrogant." Her disappointment went all the way to the bone, causing her temper to flare. "You think you know me so damn well that you can read my mind?"

Lucky didn't want to waste time fighting. Not when he could feel their stolen time together drawing to a close.

"I know that when I touch your breasts—" he cupped one in his hand and felt it swell to fit his palm "—they bloom like my mom's summer roses."

He dipped his head and kissed her temple. Her lips. The fragrant hollow of her throat. "I know when I kiss you, you melt like warm honey in my arms."

He drew her closer, fitting her against him. The buttery afternoon sun was warming the bright yellow straw beneath the blanket he'd spread out; Jude's blood turned even warmer.

"I know—"

"All right." She caught hold of his hair and dragged his roving mouth back to hers. "I concede. You *can* read my mind. Which means—" she stroked a wet swath against his bottom lip with the tip of her tongue and felt his deep shudder "—you know what I want you to do now."

"Let me guess." He drew back and looked into her eyes, so hard and deep Jude was certain he could see all the way to her soul. "You want me to make love with you."

Her answering laugh was rich with emotion, ragged with need. "What a smart man you are."

"For a cowboy hunk." He rolled over, rubbing against her in a seductive way. As he slipped inside her with silky smooth ease, it crossed Jude's mind that if they weren't careful, they were going to set the barn on fire.

Then he began to move, slowly, deeply, claiming her in all the ways a man can claim a woman, and she forgot to think at all.

SHE COULD NO longer put it off. Tycoon Mary was adamant: if Jude wasn't back in the office by Monday morning, no matter what the circulation rates on the special cowboy hunk issue turned out to be, she could kiss her job goodbye. Although Jude was willing to accept the consequences, Lucky wouldn't let her.

"You're letting your heart run away with your head, sweetheart." They were in the barn, surrounded by the scents of leather, hay and horses she knew she'd be taking back to New York in her memory. Lucky had brought her here to say their goodbyes in private.

"I've let my head rule my entire life, up until I chased after you to Wyoming, and I've never been as happy as I've been here with you. Following my heart."

"You keep talking like that and *my* head's gonna swell so big I'm going to need to go shopping for a new hat," he said. "And as good as it makes me feel to hear you say that, Jude, I'm not going to let you rush into anything."

"But—"

He touched a finger to her lips, forestalling her protest. "There's a lot to be said for patience, sweetheart. As Buck always says, given enough time, even an egg will walk."

"He also says that there's a powerful difference between a good sound reason to do something and a reason to do something that just *sounds* good." She jutted out her chin. "I like that one better."

"You never have fought fair." Affection fought with regret in his warm gaze. "If you want to start trading off Buckisms, we'll still be standing here this time next year."

"That'd be fine with me."

He shook his head. "Dammit, do you honestly think I want to put you on that plane this afternoon?"

"Then don't."

"It's the right thing to do," he insisted doggedly, as he had from the beginning. How could he explain that he was afraid to death that if he let her stay here with him, she'd end up hating the ranch and him, and breaking his heart in the bargain when she finally felt the need to return to the lights of the big city? Better to break things off clean right now, he'd decided.

"I truly do love you, Jude, but—"

"Then let me stay." Jude found herself on the verge of begging. But beg she would, if that's what it took to make him understand that her life—her future—was here at the Double Ought with him.

"Aw, darlin', if only it were that simple." He touched his forehead to hers and sighed. "I've seen other men bring women out here and within six months two people who thought they were in love were making each other miserable."

"Those men weren't you. And the women weren't me."

He'd never met a more stubborn female. Never met one who could turn him inside out the way this one could.

He was about to answer when the sound of a throat clearing drew their attention toward the open door.

"Sorry to interrupt," Zach said, his expression echoing his words. "But if we want to catch that plane, Jude, we'd better get going."

"I'll be right there," she managed to reply, wanting to cry.

"Six months," Lucky repeated after Zach had left them alone again. It was the arbitrary schedule he'd set, suspecting that she'd lose interest long before then. "Meanwhile, I'll come back east to see you—"

"That'll be the day," she muttered. "You didn't even come to see your own nephew."

"Kate was homesick. She wanted to bring Dillon back to Wyoming. But I *will* come see you. For Thanksgiving."

"Promise?"

"Absolutely." If she still wanted him by then.

Her eyes were welling up, any further words of protest clogged in her throat. She went up on her toes and pressed her lips hard against his.

Passion soared, causing her aching heart to feel as if it were going to shatter. She clung to him, needy, desperate, frustrated. Then, knowing that she'd hit the stony wall of his intransigence, knowing that nothing she could ever say would change his mind, she broke free.

"I don't want you coming to the airport with me."

Lucky saw the walls going up and wondered if he'd ever see her again. And wondered how the hell he was expected to go through life if he didn't.

"Fine." O'Neill pride kept his tone tight, his back straight when he wanted to grovel.

"I'll send you some copies of the magazine."

"Fine," he repeated.

She stared up at him, her heart in her eyes, reminding him of a wounded female fawn he'd found in the woods when he was twelve. After removing the arrow from its flank, he'd nursed it back to health, and for a while, it continued to come back to the ranch every night for the cracked corn he'd fed it. Eventually, it had stopped coming. He'd seen it a few times, grown to a doe, grazing in the woods with her own family. She'd made herself a happy life that had no longer included him.

"Damn you, Lucky. You think you always know what's best for everyone. But you are so wrong about this!"

Hating him and loving him both at the same time, Jude pulled out of his arms, whirled away and went running out of the barn.

"WANT TO GET A DRINK?" Zach asked. Thunderstorms in the area had played havoc with airline schedules and they'd already been waiting at the crowded gate an hour.

During this time Jude hadn't been able to say a word. Indeed, Michael O'Neill had driven them into town and Jude had been extremely grateful that Lucky's father was not nearly as loquacious as Buck. There'd been no way she could have carried on a polite conversation while her heart was lying in broken pieces all over the floor of the Double Ought's barn.

"Why not?" She shrugged and followed him into the nearest cocktail lounge. The TV was on. As Jude sipped her glass of white wine, her gaze drifted with disinterest up toward the screen.

"More fires," Zach murmured as they watched the deadly flames eating up the Wyoming grasslands.

Chills ran up her spine. Her fingers tightened instinctively on the stem of her glass. "Lucky said they're good for the grass."

"In the long run. But in the short term—" He broke off his answer and cursed.

Jude saw him at the same moment. It was Lucky, his face grim, being interviewed by a pretty blond newswoman clad in jeans and a western shirt.

"All we can do is try to get the stock out of the way," he was saying. "And hope that the wind changes."

"Oh, my God." Jude pressed her hand against her pounding heart as she thought about the horses, the waving fields of grass, the house. The people. The images that had tormented her in nightmares since childhood flashed in her mind as she jumped up from the bar, knocking her wooden chair over with a clatter. "I have to be with him."

She was almost out of the bar when Zach caught hold of her arm. "What the hell are you planning to do? Run all the way out to the Double Ought? In case you've forgotten, there aren't a lot of taxis that run from here to the ranch."

"Good point." Accustomed to making quick decisions, she spun back toward the bartender. "Do you own a truck?"

"Sure. Why?"

"I need to rent it."

"What?"

She dug into her purse and pulled out the crisp twenty dollar bills she'd gotten earlier from the automatic teller in the terminal. "Here's two hundred dollars. I promise I'll return it tomorrow. I just need to get out to Cremation Creek."

"What makes you think that poor excuse for a town is even going to be there tomorrow?" He flashed a glance up at the screen. "It could be nothing but ashes by morning."

Jude wanted to scream. "Here." She took off her watch. "You can keep this for collateral."

He looked at the status symbol she'd once been so proud of as if he'd never seen a watch before. "What the hell do you expect me to do with this?"

Damn. What was it about Wyoming men that made them so frustratingly stubborn? Another idea occurred to her. "Give him your cameras, Zach."

"What?"

"I said, give the man your cameras." She grabbed the case from him and plunked it onto the bar. "Believe me," she assured the bartender, "these are top of the line, probably worth even more, with all the lenses, than your truck. If we don't make it back by noon to-morrow—"

"Make it three," Zach said. He was willing to take a risk for O'Neill's sake, but there was a limit.

"All right. If we don't return your truck by three o'clock tomorrow afternoon, you can sell them, or hock them, or keep them, whatever you want. I just really need to get out to the Double Ought."

"Hell, why didn't you say that's where you wanted to go." He dug into the front pocket of his jeans and took out a key ring. "I went to high school with Lucky O'Neill. We were on the same basketball team. Took the championship our senior year."

"Isn't that wonderful." She didn't care about some long-ago high school basketball game. But the sight of that silver key made her heart sprout wings.

"It's the black Chevy Tahoe parked in the back lot." He rattled off the license plate. "You can't miss it. It's got a Frontier Days bumper sticker and a PRCA decal on the back window. That's Professional Rodeo Cow-boy's Association," he added with not a little pride.

"I know." She'd learned a lot during her too brief time in Wyoming. "Thank you." Acting on impulse, she went up on the toes of the boots Lucky's mother had insisted she keep, and kissed him on the cheek. "I promise to invite you to the wedding."

There'd been a slight argument over who'd drive. But as Jude sat in the passenger seat of the truck going ninety down the highway, she decided she was glad she'd reluctantly caved in. Her hands, as she kept punching radio buttons, seeking a news update, were shaking badly.

"He'll be all right, Jude," Zach assured her.

"I know that." She couldn't allow herself to think

otherwise. "But all his stock. And the house." At the memory of standing outside on a cold snowy night, watching another home go up in flames, she pressed her fingertips against her closed lids.

The wind had picked up; even inside the truck Jude could hear it howling. The fire had jumped the highway; the grass on both sides of the road had been scorched as black as the asphalt. The smoke they were driving through became thicker and thicker the closer they got to the Double Ought, obscuring their vision, slipping into the car through the dashboard vents, making her throat burn.

Jude had never been more afraid in her life.

"You're pale as a damn ghost," Zach complained, shooting her a worried look. "Why don't you let me take you back to the airport, then I'll go—"

"No." She shook her head and wrapped her arms around herself in a futile attempt to hold in the tremors. "I need to be with Lucky."

"Stubborn as a damn mule," he muttered the accusation she'd heard more than once from Lucky.

Jude didn't answer. She just kept watching the evil red flames that were racing ahead of them, turning the rolling landscape into a living, breathing, murderous image of hell.

They'd only gone a few miles when a thunderhead driven by the winds suddenly exploded overhead. Lightning flashed all around them, pebble-size hail began pouring from the sky, hitting the windshield like bullets, obscuring their vision even worse.

A herd of elk suddenly ran across the road in front of them. Zach slammed on the brakes, sending the truck into a skid. He cursed viciously, twisting the steering wheel, as the sound of brakes squealing rent the smoky air.

Jude held on to her seat for dear life and closed her eyes as the out-of-control spin seemed to last an eternity. They finally came to a shuddering halt, headed in the opposite direction.

"I'm impressed," she managed to gasp. They were both breathing heavily, as if they'd run miles across the burning fields. She was also extremely glad that she hadn't been driving. "I don't know how you avoided hitting one of those elk."

"Obviously our guardian angels were on duty," he muttered as a nearby bolt of lightning hit the ground with a force that actually rocked the heavy truck. "Because I sure didn't have all that much to do with it." He exchanged a long look with her, took a deep, ragged breath, then backed up, making a U-turn that headed them back toward the Double Ought.

"Aw, hell," he muttered less than five minutes later. "So, do you think Tycoon Mary will pay for our speeding ticket?"

Jude glanced back and saw the flashing lights behind them. "Just tell him you're sorry and take the ticket," she instructed. "We don't have time to try to talk our way out of it."

"Yes, ma'am," he said mildly as he pulled over to the side of the road.

"I'm sorry." Why couldn't that trooper walk a little faster? "I didn't mean to sound so bossy, it's just that I'm so worried—"

"I know." He patted her leg. "It'll be okay. He'll be okay."

"I know." Jude couldn't allow herself to believe otherwise.

Zach rolled down the window, letting in the rain, along with an acrid cloud of smoke that made them both start coughing.

"Hello, officer. I'm sorry my foot got a little heavy on the metal, but—"

"I'm not stopping you for speeding," the trooper was forced to shout over the storm. "We're blocking off the highway. You're going to have to turn back."

"Oh, no!" Jude cried out. "We can't."

"Jude," Zach warned quietly. "Let me handle this." He looked back up at the patrolman whose face was wet from the hail that was rapidly turning to a cold, pelting rain. "Are you going to arrest us if we keep driving to Cremation Creek?"

"If you cross the roadblock, I have the authority to do that. The smoke's gettin' too thick to drive safely, the hail's got the damn road as slick as ice, and there's always the danger of you getting caught in a flare-up—"

"You don't understand, officer." Jude was leaning across Zach now, desperate to plead her case. The fear of being caught in a firestorm was nothing compared to her fear of losing Lucky. "I have to get to the Double Ought."

His eyes narrowed and he shot her a serious look from beneath the wide brown brim of the plastic-covered campaign hat. "You're going out to the O'Neill place?"

"You know the O'Neills?"

"Went to school with Katie." A slight smile came to his mouth. "Had a crush on her all through our senior year, but then she went back east to college. I hear she's married now."

"Yes." She struggled to keep her raised voice reasonably calm when what she wanted to do was scream with impatience. "She and Jack are very happy. She has a baby. A boy."

"Isn't that something." He shook his head. "Little Katie bein' a mom."

"She's a wonderful mother," she assured him. "About our going to the ranch—"

"Well, hell." He rubbed his jutting chin. "Seein' as how you two are friends of the O'Neill's—"

"Oh, we're more than friends," Jude said quickly. "I'm going to be a member of the family."

"Is that so? Guess you're not talking about Buck."

As upset as she was, as dearly as she wanted to get going again, Jude managed a faint smile at that idea. "No. I'm going to marry Lucky. And you're invited to the wedding, officer."

"Sounds like a plan," he agreed. He looked at Zach. "The way I see it, there isn't much way I can stop anyone who was already on the highway before I put the barricades up."

"Oh, thank you, officer!" Jude nearly wept with relief.

"No problem." He touched his fingers to his hat. "You drive careful now," he warned Zach. "You're not going to get to the Double Ought if you roll this thing."

"I promise to take it slow," Zach answered.

"Can't ask more than that," the trooper agreed, his expression revealing that he knew that was a bald-faced lie.

"I can't believe we wasted all that time," Jude complained once they finally were on their way again. She leaned forward, staring through the black smoke and the slanting gray curtain of rain, trying to catch sight of the turnoff to the ranch. "There it is!"

This time he braked slowly, managing to make the turn. Jude was terrified anew when she saw that the fire had already taken out the grass on one side of the pitted gravel ranch road.

"You realize he might not even be there," Zach warned. "They could have evacuated."

"He wouldn't have left the horses." She'd watched him with Annie and Lightning and the others and knew that there was no way Lucky would abandon the animals he loved so well. "And if they'd gotten them all in the stock trailer, they would have passed us."

And then, finally, they were at the house, which was, miraculously, still standing. As was the barn. Heedless of her own safety, she was out of the truck before Zach managed to bring it to a full stop.

And then, through the acrid haze that made her eyes water and her throat burn, she saw them: Buck, Marianne and Michael, and, blessedly, Lucky. She called his name, then ran toward him and flung herself into his arms. His strong, wonderful arms.

"You're safe!" She was laughing and crying all at the same time.

"What the hell are you doing here?" he asked, even as he lifted her off her feet and held her tight.

"I saw you on the news and there was no way I was going to stay away. I was so worried!"

He stared at her. "You drove through all that?"

"Zach drove. I was too busy praying."

"She also refused to turn back, even when the trooper tried to block the highway," Zach divulged as he joined them.

"You realize that you're crazy." He couldn't even begin to imagine what she must have been going through. Driving through that firestorm would have been horrific enough even without her tragic personal history. Realizing that she'd risked her own life for him proved stunning.

"If anything had happened to you..." He never would have been able to forgive himself.

"Nothing was going to happen. Because I was coming to you," Jude insisted raggedly. She was grateful that he was holding her because now that the adrenaline rush was beginning to fade, her legs were turning so rubbery she doubted they'd be capable of holding her up. "My heart was already here, Lucky. What was I supposed to do without it?"

Not having the words to answer that, he kissed her, his rough lips claiming hers, branding her. When he finally released her mouth, she glanced over at the house that would need repainting, but thankfully had escaped the flames.

"I'm so relieved the house survived." It was a house made for children. Jude hoped Lucky liked the idea of a big family.

"Mom kept the hose on it while the rest of us managed to get the horses into the trailer, but we didn't need to leave, because the firebreak we made with the tractor managed to work. And, although it looked a little iffy for a while, once the rain came, we were out of the woods."

His red-veined eyes were rimmed in black; the rain had made rivers in his soot-darkened face. He was wet and filthy and he was hers. All hers. Forever and ever, amen.

"You're not sending me away, cowboy." Tears born of relief, of joy, of love, were streaming down her face. "Not this time."

He laughed, a rough release of pent-up emotion. "New York, I wouldn't even try."

One year later

"THIS IS A damn fool idea."

"Now, Buck," Jude cajoled. "Don't be so difficult." She leaned forward, adjusting the string tie. "The minute Kate came up with it, I thought the idea of putting you and Mary Lou on the cover of *Rocky Mountain Matchmaker* magazine was brilliant. After all, you were on the cover of our very first issue. And here you are, about to get married." She tilted his fawn Stetson to a rakish angle. "Think of all the subscriptions you'll get us. You're a true success story."

But not the only one. She and Kate had formulated the idea of a magazine designed to bring men and women together in the sparsely populated spaces of the mountain west. Since its launch, it had engineered five marriages, three engagements, and at least a dozen couples had reported having met their own personal Mr. or Ms. Right.

"Don't be such a hard-ass, Buck." The bride-to-be— grandmother to the Feed and Fuel's Dixie and Lila— was a tall, buxom, beautiful woman in her sixties. She stroked his cheek with her fingertips; the diamond engagement ring caught the light and split it into rainbows. "I like the idea of being on the front of Jude and Katie's magazine."

"That's the only reason I'm doin' it," he grumbled. "Because of you, darlin'."

As Buck touched his hand to Mary Lou's hair, Zach snapped the shutter, capturing the tender gesture for posterity.

As Jude wiped away the moisture from her suddenly damp eyes, she exchanged a smile with Zach and knew they were thinking the same thing. How much all their lives had changed in the past twelve months.

After shooting the Cowboy Hunk issue—which had, indeed, shattered circulation records as Jude had predicted—the photographer had returned to his home state. Within the year, he had already earned himself a reputation taking sepia photos of ranching and rodeo life. He didn't need to work for Jude, but she was grateful he continued to shoot her quarterly cover as an act of friendship.

As she'd also predicted, Tycoon Mary had fired Kate, but that had provided the impetus for her and Jack to leave the city she'd only stayed in for her husband's sake. Dillon was walking—actually, running most of the time—and his uncle had already had him on the back of a horse and proclaimed the toddler was a natural-born cowboy.

Jack seemed to be thriving in his job as vice president of a Wells Fargo Bank branch in Cheyenne. The elder Peterson, who'd discovered his social security checks stretched much further out here than they had in Manhattan, had recently taken up fishing. Mrs. Peterson had started a book group at the Cheyenne library specializing in Wyoming writers. Their current discussion centered around Mary Roberts Rineheart's *The Circular Staircase.*

"You've done good, kid," Zach murmured, sharing her thoughts as he had so often during their years together.

"I know." Her gaze shifted to the pine cradle that had been hand carved by Buck for his grandson. Six-week-old Garvey, named for the first O'Neill to settle in the lush green valley on the banks of Cremation Creek, was sleeping peacefully, his thumb stuck between his rosebud lips. "And to think, I owe it all to *Hunk of the Month.*"

And speaking of hunks...the door to the makeshift studio opened and her husband walked in, crossing the room with that lazy, loose-hipped stride that Jude knew would still have the power to make her heart hammer when she was ninety.

"Got the last of the bulls down," he announced as he gathered her in his arms. This year, rather than drive back and forth, the crew had camped out, and although he'd only been gone five days, Jude had missed him terribly. "And I couldn't wait to get home to you and the littlest cowboy, here."

Home. Had there ever been a more glorious word? Jude thought how ironic it was that she'd first come to Wyoming to save her New York publishing career, and found the home and family she'd always longed for.

"I'm glad. We've missed you."

"Not as much as I've missed you." He glanced over at his grandfather, who was, amazingly, wearing a suit, and Mary Lou who still looked damn good in an ivory lace dress that clung to her generous figure. "Can you two keep an eye on Garvey for a time?"

"Nothin' I'd love better," Buck's fiancée said promptly.

"Great." He scooped Jude up and began walking out of the room. He paused in the doorway. "Don't feel any need to hurry dinner," he advised his grandfather.

"It's my five-alarm chili." Buck grinned. "It'll keep."

"Great."

"That's the nice thing about five-alarm chili," Jude

said on a merry laugh as he carried her up the stairs to the spacious addition they'd added onto the house after their marriage. "The longer it simmers, the better it gets."

"Then believe me, darlin', it's going to get to be champion, blue-ribbon quality tonight," Lucky promised as he kicked the bedroom door closed behind him.

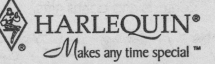

It's hot...
and it's out of control!

**This summer, Temptation turns up the heat.
Look for these bold, provocative,
ultra-sexy books!**

#686 SEDUCING SULLIVAN
Julie Elizabeth Leto
June 1998

Angela Harris had only one obsession—Jack Sullivan.
Ever since high school, he'd been on her mind...and
in her fantasies. But no more. At her ten-year
reunion, she was going to get him out of her system
for good. All she needed was one sizzling night with
Jack—and then she could get on with her life.
Unfortunately she hadn't counted on Jack having a
few obsessions of his own....

BLAZE! Red-hot reads from

DEBBIE MACOMBER

invites you to the

HEART OF TEXAS

Join Debbie Macomber as she brings you the lives
and loves of the folks in the ranching community
of Promise, Texas.

If you loved Midnight Sons—don't miss
Heart of Texas! A brand-new six-book series
from Debbie Macomber.

Available in February 1998
at your favorite retail store.

Heart of Texas by Debbie Macomber

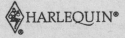

HARLEQUIN®

HPHRT1

HARLEQUIN®

Temptation®

COMING NEXT MONTH

#685 MANHUNTING IN MISSISSIPPI Stephanie Bond
Manhunting...

Piper Shepherd, the only single member of her sorority, was going to find a husband—or else. But the pickin's *were* pretty slim in Mudville, Mississippi, population twenty! Then a gorgeous stranger arrived in town. Piper thought she'd found Mr. Right—until she noticed his ring....

#686 SEDUCING SULLIVAN Julie Elizabeth Leto
Blaze

Angela Harris had only one obsession—Jack Sullivan. Ever since high school he'd been on her mind...and in her fantasies. But no more. At her ten-year reunion, she was going to get him out of her system for good! One steamy night with Jack—and then she could get on with her life. Unfortunately, she hadn't counted on Jack having a few obsessions of his own....

#687 DREAMS Rita Clay Estrada

Greg Torrance was a dream come true for Mary Ellen Gallagher. Not only was he tall, dark *and* handsome, but he offered her big money for the work she loved to do! The nightmare began when she fell in love with her sexy client—only to discover his heart belonged to someone else...whether he knew it or not.

#688 A DIAMOND IN THE ROUGH Selina Sinclair
Sara Matthews had to find an impressive date for the party where her ex-fiancé would announce his engagement to another woman. Dark, mysterious Dakota Wilder was *perfect*. Dakota hated parties, but he did fancy Sara, so they struck an outrageous deal. He'd find her a date...if she let him seduce her!

AVAILABLE NOW:

#681 MANHUNTING IN MIAMI
Alyssa Dean

#682 PRIVATE FANTASIES
Janelle Denison

#683 HUNK OF THE MONTH
JoAnn Ross

#684 ENTICING EMILY
Gina Wilkins